First published in Great Britain in 2008 by Comma Press
www.commapress.co.uk

'I Cannot Cross Over' first published in *Hyphen* (Comma 2003), 'Tabs' in *Newcastle Stories 1* (Comma 2004), 'The Custodian' in *Phantoms at the Phil: the First Proceedings* (Side Reel Press 2005), 'Three Fevers' and 'Kiss Me Deadly on the Museum Island' in *Ellipsis 1* (Comma 2005), 'It Follows Therefore' in *Phantoms at the Phil: the Second Proceedings* (Side Reel Press 2006), and The Cricket Match at Green Lock and The Silence Room in *Phantoms at the Phil: the Third Proceedings* (Side Reel Press 2007). 'Three Fevers' was also broadcast on BBC Radio 4 in October 2005.

Lines from 'Mr Bleaney' by Philip Larkin, from THE COLLECTED POEMS published Faber & Faber, 2003. Reprinted by permission of Faber and Faber Ltd.

A CIP catalogue record of this book is available from the British Library.

ISBN   1905583176
ISBN-13   978 1905583171

The publisher gratefully acknowledges assistance from the Arts Council England North West, and also the support of Literature Northwest.

Set in Bembo 11/13 by David Eckersall
Printed and bound in England by SRP Ltd, Exeter

THE SILENCE ROOM

by
Sean O'Brien

In Memory of Chrissie Glazebrook

Contents

I Cannot Cross Over

After Antonio Tabucchi

'You don't want to go down there, pet,' she said, pausing in the mouth of the lane. 'Come in here for a nice drink with me.' Beyond her I could see the beer signs through the windows of the bar.

'Sorry but I can't,' I said. 'I'm supposed to be elsewhere.'

'What's that got to do with owt? Come on.'

The bells of the cathedral church began to toll, sending mass flights of starlings racing over the old town. The light was taking on the neon edge it gets at six o'clock in summer. It was the magic hour for freezing lager and pepper vodka.

'Sorry.'

'You won't get a better offer.'

'I know, it's just —'

'Suit yerself. Bloody poets.' And she was gone with a clatter of heels over the cobblestones. I couldn't remember how we'd fallen into conversation. Maybe walking down from the Metro station at Monument. Maybe she asked for a look at my paper. It didn't matter. I liked her with her piled up dyed blonde hair, I liked the frankness of her manner and her cleavage. But I had to be elsewhere. You know how it is, in the middle of things.

I turned off into Pudding Chare. What would her name be? I saw clearly — and maybe it was true - that she was called Lorraine and that by day she worked on a cosmetics counter in Fenwicks, wearing terra cotta make-up. It seemed a strangely romantic life to me at that moment, though

1

doubtless filled with the normal obstructions and sadness.

As I hurried on I looked into the window of a bar round the back of the newspaper offices, a place once used by print workers. There was already half a crowd in there – blonde girls, their heads averted, none of them precisely her.

On the steps of the Lit and Phil Library I met Bobby the caretaker sweeping up the glass from a broken sherry bottle. Bobby was a naturalised Aberdonian. His expression always indicated that his suspicions were being confirmed.

'You're late the night,' he said.

'But not too late, I hope.'

He studied his watch.

'Well. No. But divvent fuck about. Miss Quine is long away and I want to get a good seat in the Innisfree. For the exotics.' He winked, like a lustful automaton. I imagined his female equivalent in her pinny and headscarf sliding stiffly out of the door behind him on her track, while he was drawn back into the darkness.

'I just need to check something.'

'Aye, well, it's a library,' he said, and turned back to his sweeping.

In the main gallery the three girls at the issue desk sat reading and fiddling with their long fair hair, perched on stools like mermaids on their rocks. None of them looked up as I passed – I could have been anyone – but I heard a faint echoing *tut* as I reached the doors at the far end. Was I a nuisance? I was a member. I went down the stone staircase, past paintings of the nineteenth century magistrates and antiquarians who had nurtured the library towards its present sepia perfection. None of these long-gone gentlemen would meet my eye just now.

The Silence Room is a place I do not care for. It is a brown chamber crowded with stacks of county records from the eighteenth and nineteenth centuries, as well as some impractically narrow tables at which anorexic pedants sometimes crouch to labour. It feels like an abandoned work by M.R. James. Bad enough on a spring evening when the light comes faintly down the crack between the library and the Coroner's Court and through the crusty window. Unthinkable on a foggy winter night.

All I knew was there was meant to be something in there for me to collect, perhaps a message. Where would you hide something in a library? Not among the books, surely. That could lead to misunderstanding: you might mistake a scribbled execration for the message. You could end up standing there, pondering the meaning of *nonsense* or *shite*.

I paced the parquet floor, wondering where to look. Fortunately the pedants had all gone home, leaving only the faintest tremor of disapproval. I felt beneath the tables each in turn, in case there was something stuck there with gum or worse. Nothing. But I couldn't simply leave: where would I go? I cast around, at a loss, then noticed, not for the first time, that the grille covering the radiator beneath the window had been loosened, as if in some incomplete act of maintenance or vandalism. Now I put my hand inside. The sudden heat shocked me. I was feeling awkwardly around when I heard a voice.

'Now then you dorty fucker. Get yer hand oot of its arse man.'

'What?'

'I'm not surprised yer fuckin deef neither.'

It was the poet Ralph Cowan. He was a drunk. In fact he was more of a drunk than a poet, though his real vocation was heckling. His jacket sagged to one side under the weight of a bottle. He brandished a ham and pease pudding sandwich in one hand; in the other he waved a sheet of paper.

'Yer looking fer this, reet.' Ralph was in his pomp.

'What is it?'

'Fucked if I knaa, canny lad.'

Suddenly indifferent, he handed me the paper. On it was typed, 'I cannot cross over.'

'That's a quotation from the great storehouse of local song and story,' he said, examining his sandwich. 'As ye would knaa if ye was from round here.'

'I do know, Ralph.'

'Not properly. Wouldn't be possible that.'

I looked at the line of typing again. The typewriter ribbon was worn, with both the red and black strands showing through.

'Ye gannin fer a drink?'

'Not with you.'

'Ya cunt. Go on.'

'No thanks.'

'Go on, cunt. Call yerself a poet? Howay man, what about the republic of fuckin letters, man?'

'I'm busy. Let me through the door, Ralph. Don't make me knack you.' He stepped aside.

'Busy? Aye, writin more daft radio shite about Collingwood's monument. Aboot which ye knaa fuckin fuck all by the way. ' He followed me halfway up the stairs. 'No need to be stand-offish, like.'

Back in the gallery I could hear the drumming of rain on the glass dome above. How quickly the weather had changed. Seeing Ralph's familiar brown hooded mackintosh on the coat stand by the coffee hatch, I slipped it on and left without a second glance.

When I came out on to the street I had a sudden sense of the urgency of my situation. Wherever I was meant to go, and for whatever purpose I was meant to go there, I needed to be making better progress. Now there was torrential rain, with thunder unrolling overhead. Crowds of girls in next to nothing ran shrieking over the road between hydroplaning taxis. A drayman's horse had been struck by lightning and lay smoking and hissing on a zebra crossing while its owner stamped and raved in the flooded gutter and passengers emerging from the railway station rushed past with umbrellas and briefcases raised like the accused on their way into court. A police car nosed slowly through the crush. I thought: I must write it all down when I get chance.

In this town everything gravitates towards the Quayside, so I decided to let physics take its course. But then as I made for the steps beside the ruined castle keep I saw the lights of the bar at the entrance to the high bridge. I didn't want to drink with Ralph Cowan, but I could certainly do with a refreshing beverage. And perhaps, with chance to reflect, my thinking would be clarified. Once through the doors, though, the signs were bad. The place was heaving with lawyers talking at the tops of their voices. I ordered a pint of stout and took a seat in the brown mirrored gloom of a bay as far as possible from the crowd.

What now? I thought. I could simply sit there and smoke cigarettes and drink beer on the off chance that something would happen. Waves of new lawyers came in, loud with triumph and worldly wisdom. Gradually they spilled backwards from the bar area, preening and jabbering until all I could see were their expensive corvine backsides. I looked down in despair. Under my glass was a crudely printed leaflet. I examined it. *Poetry Workshop*, it said. *Upstairs, tonight.*

I couldn't remember how long ago it was since last I climbed the sticky treads of that narrow staircase. The memory was both immediate and remote, like a first visit to the dentist. There was a sweet sick smell of beer and smoke. At the first turning I nearly collided with a woman in a red PVC raincoat. She pushed past me, putting on a pair of sunglasses, weeping, swearing under her breath. It was always a hard school, I thought, but tonight's workshop could barely have got started.

I slipped through the door and peered through the pall of smoke in the Function Room. A dozen participants of all ages sat with bowed heads at the little tables, writing furiously on lined pads. At the front of the group stood Walter

Demarest, high priest of the Beginners' Group – a gaunt grey man with an eyepatch and a thermos flask. It was, he gave people to understand, his manifest destiny to issue weekly disappointments to his obedient secular flock. They would thank him in the end. He had a plate in his head.

'You can't come in.' he said. 'You're not a member.' Then, recognising me, he muttered, 'Got summat for you.' He began to search one of the many carrier bags of manuscripts and magazines and small press publications which surrounded his table. 'Brought it with me, I know that.'

'What is it?'

'In a manila envelope.' He continued ferreting. Everyone had stopped to watch. Some of them took the chance to dab their faces with Kleenex. 'Got it,' Walter said at last. He handed me a stiff seven by five manila envelope. Nothing was written on it. The group waited.

'Open it, then,' said someone.

'How do I know it's for me?'

'She told me it was,' said Walter.

'Who did?'

'Dunno. Some French bird. Blonde.'

Not French, I thought, but Belgian. Zsa Zsa Maeterlinck. At last.

'We haven't got all day,' said Walter. 'We're only booked till eight.'

I opened the envelope. Inside was a single black garter trimmed with red.

'O-ho!' said someone.

'Best be off,' I said.

'Aye,' said Walter. 'Some of us have got poems to write.'

By now a heavy fog had rolled in up the river. The traffic tiptoed off the bridge and the drunks tiptoed under the traffic. I don't know why, but I felt my way along a wall of glazed white brick until I found a gap and skated down a cobbled alleyway into a back court surrounded by stooped and ancient solicitors' offices. Only the stairwells were lit now, their grades of desolation rising to the dim yellow spaces under the roofs, where the lifts turned back and the cares of innumerable forgotten lives lay stacked in manila folders, awaiting the attentions of rot. This was something else I was going to have to get round to writing about, afterwards, whenever that might be.

Melancholy overtook me now. I could taste the fog, as though I were breathing through the woollen scarf my mother had made me wear as a child. It had a stony, watery, acrid taste. It was like something official which everyone had mistakenly assumed was long gone into exile. It was like the first day at school. I felt afraid.

Another entryway led me into a street with flooded gutters, running beneath the viaduct, a place of informal archway garages and of erotic assignations conducted on a similar economic basis. The yellow mouth of a pub leered out of the gloom, so I went in. The bar was empty, but there was the loud steady noise of many voices somewhere in the building. Behind the bar a calendar showed Miss September, Zsa Zsa Materlinck wearing a smile and a garter. I noticed that the year she represented contained only nine months. Time was pressing

'Private party,' said the florid, brilliantined manager, emerging through the smoke, his tooth glinting to match his tiepin. He twirled a gold Albert hanging on a chain from his waistcoat, and nodded towards the hatch. 'Funeral, like. Stout, is it?'

A barmaid with a face like a large red fish in a beehive hairdo leaned through the hatch.

'We need some more crabsticks, Maurice,' she said.

'What do they fockin dee with 'em aal?' the gaffer said. 'Have you ever seen anyone actually eating one?' he asked me.

I tried to look noncommittal. But really I knew where

the crabsticks went – down the cracks of the plush benches at funeral buffets.

'Whose do is it?'

'Dennis Foot. Ye knaa him?'

'I know of him.' Dennis Foot was the legendary angling correspondent of the *Argus*. He too had been a poet. And now he was gone to his long home. Or perhaps they would bury him at sea, or burn him like a Viking. I struggled to find anything to add to this thought. Call yourself a poet?

Eventually I asked, 'What did he die of?'

'Seafood poisoning,' said the manager. 'Never touch it meself like.'

The barmaid came through with a new tray of crabsticks.

'Go on, pet, since you're here.'

'I'm a vegan.'

'We're very broadminded. Hang on. You're him. Aren't you?'

'Perhaps I'm not the person you should ask.'

'I've gorra note from your pal.'

I couldn't remember having any pals. I couldn't remember being in this pub, or this pub being here before.

'The skinny one. Wears a coat.' She took a betting slip from her bosom and handed it to the manager. He looked at me carefully, then put on a pair of spectacles and read the note:

'"The river is wide but I cannot."' What's that supposed to mean, like?'

'Hard to say.'

'Sounds bloody daft,' said the barmaid. 'Vegan, right?' She exchanged glances with the manager.

'I could show you me poems if you want, like', he said, shyly.

'Actually I'm a bit pressed now.'

He carefully took off his spectacles and re-pocketed them in his waistcoat.

'Word to the wise,' he said.

'Of course.'

'Yer barred.'

Back in the fogbound night a coal train crawled past, high overhead, adding its rusty black sweat to the fog. Press on, I thought. The viaduct curved away and quiet fell. Now the street was edged with metal fencing topped with razor wire. I had heard of this place but never visited it before. The Cultural Quarter. A gate stood open. I picked my way across the rubble and rags to a low concrete building which felt as if it stood at the edge of a cliff. It was the kind of place the army would have used as a venereal clinic. In fact it was the premises of a publisher. The door swung open. So this was my pal. Neville Maddox.

'Been a while,' he said, extending a cold white hand from the overlong sleeve of his dark overcoat.

'I wasn't expecting you,' I said. 'I thought you were dead.'

'That's rather an emotive term,' said Neville. He offered me his hipflask. I declined. As he tipped his head back there came the faint pang of vodka, not a smell, just a rumour, one for the columns of Intimations in the *Argus*. Neville led me inside. The front office contained nothing but old catalogues. The storeroom held only old ladder-style shelving. Beyond both lay the editor's office. This too was empty, except that in the middle of the floor stood a wooden pallet bearing several stacks of shrink-wrapped calendars. One package had been ripped open. Neville handed me a sample. Zsa Zsa was still smiling. The garter, I now saw, was part of a pre-Christmas theme, matching her hat.

'So what happened? Where's all the poetry?'

'Pulped. Turned into these.' He flicked through the slick pages. The muses addressed their compliant smirks to eternity.

'The culture turned against us, that's what. Or the

9

economy. Or both. Or they're the same. Or something. Anyway, there was no call for these either.'

'All a bit valedictory.' I said.

'You what? We're past all that.'

I looked at the calendar. Miss May in her green scarf reached across the void to Zsa Zsa, her September cousin.

'No chance of any royalties, anyway,' said Neville, looking at his watch. 'It would appear the guvnor's fucked off. Fancy a drink?

'I've got to be somewhere.'

'That's what they all say. Where are you headed?'

'The quayside, I think. That's where I've been trying to get to all night.'

'Ahuh? I'll come down with you.'

It was sleeting through the fog as we picked our way down the steps between the wrecked nineteenth century warehouses beloved of alkies and the producers of costume dramas about the nobility of toil. Fires burned in a few rooms half-open to the air. Dim figures reclined and howled or held out brown bottles which we politely refused.

'You're ready then,' said Neville, as we reached the foot of the steps, where the bass-heavy judder of music could be heard.

'Am I?'

'Why else would you be here?'

'I'm not with you.'

'Then why'd you come?' He shook his head.

'Am I supposed to know?'

At last we came out on the street. It was crowded with the usual drinkers, groups and singletons passing silently through the music along the potholed road, slowing the night traffic along the quays. Faces I knew raised bottles in recognition and moved expressionlessly on. The sleet had turned to snow, the broad, unhurried flakes landing on the men's bald heads and the women's naked shoulders.

'I'll leave you here,' said Neville. He hailed a girl who stood in the red doorway of a bar. She waved back and went inside.

'What am I meant to do?' I asked.

He shrugged, shook my hand coldly again, then slipped over the road as the crowd thickened about him.

I let myself be drawn along with the drinkers. An eddy carried me to the river's edge, where I stopped to lean on the railings and looked down into the black waters. They were high tonight. The tide was running swiftly away, parting smoothly at the high bridge-pillars, bearing a mass of branches aloft like antlers. Among the branches, pages from the calendar surfaced – all Zsa Zsa - and were snatched below. Then, slowly, but without slowing, the water grew smooth as a mirror. My face appeared in it, with the moon on one shoulder and another face to balance it. I spoke to the figure in the water.

'You don't live here.'

'I don't live anywhere. That's the trouble, son.' The figure drew deeply on a cigarette and breathed out smoke into his white hair..

'Well, I can't help you now.'

'I know that, son,' my father said. 'Nor I you.'

'Why does it have to be you?'

He smiled bitterly. I saw the handsome devil he had been.

'Perhaps it's an ordeal.'

'Ordeals are normally rewarded,' I said.

'Are they? Are you sure? Then perhaps I'm your reward. Walk with me anyway.' He turned and threw his cigarette into the water. But when I looked up there was no one beside me. The crowds had thinned out, too. The swing bridge was open and stragglers made their way up the approaches. The waters stood still as a sealed pool, in perfect black silence. There was no sound of voices, no breaking glass, no distant traffic in the streets above the quays. The music had ended, and one by one the lights along the quay went out. I looked around for my father, for Bobby, for any companion to come with me over the bridge. All gone.

'It can't be as important as this, whatever it is,' I said.

By the time I stepped on to the bridge there was only the moon's cold lamp, with a face I liked to think was Zsa Zsa Maeterlinck's, with the snow falling into the water, and by this light I saw quite clearly that this was a river with only one side.

Tabs

The printed notice on the big table at the far end of the library was so discreet you might have thought it referred to something mundane, like the Easter closing hours – the kind of information the members acquired by osmosis anyway. In fact it stated that from March 31st – 'in line with trends elsewhere in society in general' - smoking would be banned in the library.

Change and decay in all around I see. Surely, though, the library wasn't subject to the same processes and historical forces as 'elsewhere'. It was the *library*: an ancient institution where you had to pay a subscription to join, supposing the committee's inquisitors judged you fit for membership. If all went well and you got past the caretaker and up the stone stairs you were safe in 1964, or 1958, or, if you preferred, 1913, when all the world smoked. The authority of 'elsewhere' was suspended: that was the point. *Smoking*, and smoking-affiliated activities like sitting around, like waiting, like passing the time between one thing finished and the next beginning – these, not reading and writing, gave the library its *raison d'etre*. It was a smoking library – damn few others like it anywhere. And now the lights were going out all over Europe.

There had been a time when the smoking ban would have meant a row. There would have been resignations and calls for extraordinary meetings. And, though it would have made no difference to the outcome, there would have been impassioned mutterings around the big table. It was the headquarters of a *salon des refuses* of the law and the academy. This shifting group of desperate men clung to the idea of house-ownership and the life of the mind by their fingertips there at the smoky hub of the library, like Balzacian gamblers leaving the wheel of their ruined fortunes only to drink and to pawn their last possessions. The fraternity of the big table passed the days by looking at the nudes in *Practical Photography*, rolling cigarettes and writing endless letters of application to ever more obscure law firms and institutions of higher education. Their low chorus of dissent could be heard as a reassuring background, however far away you sat. Even in the remote monastic setting of the Silence Room in the sub-basement among the county archives they could be heard, like a warning in a foreign language. Now, I realised, they too were gone, somehow – never noticed them go – and in a week or two smoking would be gone as well. The library was much too quiet.

What would remain, at least for a time, were the oily encrustations which had grown slowly, like black reefs of disease, over the books shelved in the upper galleries. You could find all sorts up there where the poets went to die – early Auden, MacNeice, Empson, alongside historical curiosities with local connections like Michael Roberts (Longbenton) and Francis Scarfe (South Shields). There was even, mysteriously, an original 1923 edition of Wallace Stevens's *Harmonium*: upstairs, it sweated tar like Eliot's Thames. By and large the diseased yellow air of these autumnal upper galleries was the haunt of librarians. They shifted the smoke-ravaged stock from shelf to shelf, like nineteenth century doctors sending their doomed consumptive patients from spa to spa. Among the sufferers were Mann's *The Magic Mountain* and Katherine Mansfield's stories – sick books that no one read now or cared to be reminded of, shunted off to heaven's gate and replaced by crime novels and lite lit for lowbrow ladies. It is of course unfair to associate the decline of smoking with the death of the educated general reader: after all, one is a fact and the other merely a suspicion, and all they have in common is simultaneity. But still. Anyway, the chances were you could get hold of the Wallace Stevens if you cared to ascend the wrought-iron spiral staircase into the previous century. Then, one day, *Harmonium* wasn't there.

It was down on the big table, it turned out, lying unopened next to a packet of tobacco, some licorice Rizlas and a cigarette lighter in the shape of a u-boat conning tower. The saturnine Harry Box was looking at the book as he rolled a cigarette. He continued to look at the book as he lit the cigarette. He renewed his scrutiny as he exhaled the first drag.

'Are you using that?' I asked.

'Ahuh.'

'I mean the copy of *Harmonium.*'

'Ahuh.'

I picked up the *TLS* and waited. A couple of years later, he glanced up and said: '*Fill your black hull / With white moonlight. // There will never be an end / To this droning of the surf.*' He seemed to expect a reply.

'Stevens.'

'Course it is.'

'From *Harmonium.*'

'Course it is.'

There seemed to be no way forward from here. Harry looked a shade disappointed.

'Tell you what.'

'Yes?'

'It's fuckin' mint, mind. Whatever any cunt says.'

To the best of my knowledge, no cunt had disparaged Stevens lately. It took me a moment to recognise, in the present context, an example of the pre-emptive aggression, directed at imagined slights, which characterises this fascinating part of the country. Honour satisfied, Harry rose and put his papers into his carrier bag, along with the copy of *Harmonium,* then left the building. He did not stop to check the book out at the issue desk. *Harmonium* may have been the property of the library, but it was Harry Box who really owned it. When I had used the book before, it had merely been on loan from Harry. I was intrigued.

Harry Box was sometimes physically in but never professionally *of* the Applicants Anonymous group at the big table. For one thing he had a job – some undefined lecturing post at a college south of the river – politics or history, I never knew exactly. Secondly, he was a rarity – a smoker who read. Attired in his patented gloom, wearing the aromatic pall of his steady consumption, he continued to quote Stevens spontaneously from time to time over the next few years. These occasions were like Bank Holidays in a Trappist monastery. *Ramon Fernandez, tell me if you can...The world is ugly and the people are sad...Upon a hill in Tennessee.* He delivered a line, then seemed to listen to it fading in time, smiling through his smoke as if it pleased him that this was the case. Thus we approached the Millennium – the ageing youths and Harry and myself, riding the table like a raft while storms elsewhere consumed unlucky mariners by the shipload.

Like many men of a certain age, out in the badlands, a few years short of forty, Harry made a big performance of the hand-rolled cigarette. He made it into an *activity*. For the duration of the making, until he nipped off a couple of loose threads of *Old Hawser*, or whatever he was smoking that week, you believed him: this was the preface to something decisive; a deed was imminent, of which all this fadge was simply the herald. Rolling a cigarette was more than a way of occupying the meantime; it was substantial and meaningful behaviour. It spoke for a world, the one at which Harry gestured through the smoke as he breathed it out in rings: the world of Stevens and the library, the bridges and the river that ran darkly beneath them, of the river's mouth and the vast satisfactory distances beyond, from here to either pole and on to Singapore and Valparaiso. Even Harry's moustache was involved in the smoke somehow, and thus in that wider world where the atlas was mainly blue, where yawning depths were crossed by vessels with Harry's rolling tobacco secreted in their bilges, like contraband. God, the man could smoke.

One day he put an open book down on the table in front of me.

'Look at that.'

I read where his yellow finger pointed: *Take a last turn / In the tang of possibility.*'

'That's what I mean,' he said. 'Do you know what I mean?'

'I think so.'

'I wanted to be a ship's navigator. I took the vision test. Turned out I was colour blind.' He smiled through the smoke, closed the copy of Heaney's *Wintering Out* and went back to reading Stevens. You could feel the globe waiting, still patient, for someone to cross it, for Harry to give up his self-possession and simply *go*. Colour blindness was only a setback. There were other means of travel. *Tout est luxe, calme et volupte.* Surely there was time. I was anxious for Harry's sake that this should be the case: anxious, I mean, that the imagination should be vindicated in its travels. For around the same time, equally unexpectedly, he showed me a handful of poems.

Normally this is a signal to make one's excuses and leave, if necessary starting a new life in a different part of the country. Beware of trespassing in the realm of green ink and alternative spelling, where the obsessed are waiting to waylay you with their lives' work. But Harry's poems were interesting. They drew on the Baudelaire of 'Le Voyage', on Rimbaud and Conrad and RLS and other seagoing literature of all kinds – and of course on Stevens, who, like Harry, never went anywhere, certainly never Abroad. Harry had Stevens's feel for the exotic. He could find it in the dancers – 'exotics' with the glottal 't' – in the clubs on Shields Road on Sunday lunchtimes, where Stevens probably would not; but Harry

17

also understood the power of names: Tehuantepec, Valparaiso, Far Cathay, planted like a path of islands, further and further into the ocean. (*Where mind and ocean meet.* I realised that where other people had conversation, Harry had quotation and reference.) The combination of longing and pre-emptive disappointment had something of Laforgue about it, but at bottom it was all his own. It was as if in any encounter he had always just cast off, back into the smoke-filled Sargasso of his seemingly unshakeable preoccupations, steered by the self-possession whose one command was *not yet*; *manana*. His mode of conversation was always, I see now, the farewell.

We fell into the habit – I'm not sure exactly how or when – of drinking together on Wednesdays when the library closed early. We crossed the river by the High Level Bridge to sit among the resonant desolation and imminent violence of the Coffin Bar. We re-crossed the water to perform what Harry called 'a sector crawl', along the quayside as the developers took aim at its dozen old blokes' bars, or wandered up behind the hospital and into the fringes of the West End, where wise men always went equipped but literary types were safe because ignored. Our conversation was simple, repetitive and – to me – intensely pleasurable. It took in Wallace Stevens, Baudelaire, Rimbaud, modernism and the sea. Harry, I recognise now, said very little. He would launch a sentence, a quotation, an allusion, down the slipway of the evening and watch as it drifted from view. The evenings dissolved like smoke in the contemplation of fragments and gnomic apercus. It was with Harry that I developed a taste for Scotch, a dark mild made from the scrapings of ashtrays and the urine of smokers. When we were getting drunk, Harry would say, 'Out there, out there,' gesturing at the bar-room door or the gantry or the dartboard, but meaning the ocean, the immense, the sublime, the all-consuming dimension where the mind could drink, drown and be re-born at eternal leisure. The riches of those absconders' hours! Sometimes a withered glass collector in a Cyrenians' suit would nod agreement at one of Harry's sudden announcements and suddenly tell us that he had been regimental bantamweight champion, that he had caught a spectacular disease in Port Said, that he had fathered a child on a black woman in Durban and always meant to go back. Harry would nod: here was proof of all he intended. He would roll the man a cigarette and then suddenly we would be out in the street, walking briskly despite being half-cut. When I asked why, Harry would say: 'He's that unhappy.'

Harry was engaged, it seemed, to a primary school teacher, Anne. She remained a misty, notional figure. She was never the direct subject of his discourse: she only emerged as sort of grammatical necessity, with consequences for other kinds of statement, referred to in terms of having to go home eventually from whichever pub we had gone to when the library closed. Relations between the sexes seemed almost unrevised hereabouts in those days: men were selfish and women complained. It took a long time for people to realise that they could manage these roles independently. When they finally did, almost overnight entire streets ceased to have a male population. A female quiet of afternoon television commenced, broken only by the weekend departures of children with overnight bags. You saw them climbing into cars whose drivers preferred not to approach the house.

But that is to anticipate. Anne was a distant, more or less benevolent idea. I imagined her as a grown-up Grace Darling, ready in her mackintosh on playground duty to do the right thing if called upon. Even though I scarcely met her, like Harry she seemed in some way already historical, a beckoning figure in the rainy doorway of The Bridge or The Crown Posada or The Barking Dog, there to extract her man, with weary good humour, from the smoke-filled room of his choice and – dare one say it – his real affections.

'She seems nice,' I said.

'Aye, canny.'

Of course, we know nothing of other people's

relationships, not really: so we tell ourselves. So I told myself that Harry's taciturn Geordismo was simply that, not an evasion of me (why need he bother? We were simply drinking companions), still less of his own life and of Anne. The mood I glimpsed between them was never of entrapped sadness on his part or of equally entrapped hopefulness on hers. Ignore that clock: the kind of time it marked was not the sort that Anne and Harry lived in. How could it be? The world was furnished with Stevens and Baudelaire – though admittedly I never found out what Anne preferred to read, supposing she did (there are people who – this is unimaginable, isn't it? – get by very well with scarcely a thought for language).

Anyway, Anne was to remain someone I never quite met. Although she came to fetch Harry several times, we were scarcely even on terms of glancing recognition when she disappeared back into the city to which she was, if anything, even more wedded than Harry was. If there was a problem, which of course there wasn't, it was that Harry was never wedded to her.

The problem was the other woman. I met her half a dozen times before I realised she *was* the other woman and not a colleague of Harry's or a friend of Anne's. Natalie would turn up in the pub or just happen to be there when we arrived. The contrast with Ann was so glaring as to be invisible, if you see what I mean. Where Ann was a pale, slight pastoral figure who should have been running a school for twelve children in the depths of Northumberland, Natalie was a creature of the city – a stilettoed blonde with crackling nylons and a voice like an icepick. Where Ann stood for patience, Natalie was all business, here, now and the next thing. Anne didn't smoke; Natalie favoured some blue-skinned, gold-tipped breed of tabs. They seemed to manufacture themselves in her tiny white handbag, into which she had evidently poured the entire contents of Wicksteeds' perfume department, where, I was not surprised to learn, she was employed in a supervisory capacity which seemed to involve standing about in a significant manner. I was only surprised that Harry should know her. She didn't strike me as a reader. Perhaps they had been at school together. Harry seemed, insofar as one could read these things, happy enough to see her. He would offer her a roll-up. She would shake her head and go on talking.

Natalie's world was full of doors she was just about to open, leading to further perfumed chambers and further exciting doors, and so on — a kind of opium dream of perpetual product launches, designed by Yves St. Laurent and Revlon. She was never stopping, only looking in, about to have to go to some unnamed but musky, darkly glittering venue. Yet her brief appearances were extremely flexible vis-a-vis the clock: Elizabeth and Helena and Coco and the rest clearly didn't mind being kept waiting. At the end of the night, when the city had once more turned into a zoo and I was aiming myself at the gaping hell-mouth of the Metro steps, Natalie would be talking about going on the Boat. The lure of this defunct cruise ship parked in the river escaped me. It had a revolving dancefloor and a legendary smell of sick. I left them to it. It is only now, in the deserts of Afterwards, that I make the connections: between Natalie and Jeanne Duval, Baudelaire's mysterious odalisque; between the local reputation of the staff of Wicksteeds' cosmetic department as part-time but vastly skilled courtesans and the cloying, imprisoning Parisian demi-monde which was the obverse of the infinite imagined ocean. Natalie was banging Harry's brains out.

Not knowing there was a crisis, I left Harry to it. Not that he would have asked for help or counsel. Not that I could have offered either. Aside from his genetic disinclination to talk about such things, our companionship was established on the basis of literary speculation. Life — that is to say, choice, responsibility, consequences — could not be permitted to intrude. That went without saying. You might object: how typically male, to overvalue — what? The pristine condition of something that in most circles would barely have qualified as conversation – *and to do so in defiance of a summons from life itself, i.e. Anne and/or Natalie.* How little you know, dear reader, if that is your view. Is there to be no space left for idleness and dreams, for the old boys' El Dorado? The Cythera of cancelled futurity?

I think, now, that Harry scarcely recognised his predicament: it was just how things went on, in the permanent meantime. But change was at hand. I noticed during the autumn that he was smoking readymades: Bensons, Silk Cut, nameless brands from backstreet minimarts – all of which he had previously treated with a hand-roller's studied contempt. He was lighting another before the first was finished. More than once I saw him look in disgusted bafflement at what he was smoking. How had things come to this, that life prevented him making his weekly visit to the bespoke tobacconist near the pawnbroker's shop to refurbish his supplies of Old Sumatra or Celebes Select? With the decline in the quality of smoking, so the ocean of his literary contemplations began to shrink.

There was nothing I could say. Harry's time – his world – was no longer his own, it seemed. He developed a hacking cough and struggled to mount Dog Leap Stairs on the way up from the quayside. He was often absent from the library. He altered then failed to keep drinking arrangements, or turned up very late, flustered, gasping, speechless. He staggered into the library one night, already well served by the look of him. He lowered himself into his usual seat at the big table and produced a silver hip-flask from an inside pocket. I declined the proffered shot. He emptied the flask, lit a Berkeley, put his head in his hands and said, in a voice I had never heard before, a voice from *outside* the library: 'Baudelaire's *Intimate Journals*, right? "Today I felt myself brushed by the wing of madness." I should fuckin coco. I'm fucked, man. That's the top and bottom of it. Fucked. The fuckin bitches have fuckin fucked me. Dunno where I am. Lost with all fuckin hands. Time to make smoke and disguise the heading.

The Black fuckin Spot's on its way. '

For a moment I was so startled I could not tell where the quotation ended and Harry began. I remember sitting there at the ashy table with my pen poised over the *TLS* crossword. This was a final leavetaking. Harry's world was being stripped of its rhetorical furnishings. All that remained was a bare unhappiness, about which there was nothing – forgive me, Tolstoy – to be said. Harry nodded, as if reading my thoughts.

'I'll catch you in the library,' he said, and walked away. Not until I heard the door swing shut did I look up. *We live, as we dream, alone.* A literary education is a wonderful thing: you need never be at a loss for the *mot juste*.

What happened next was unclear. From what I can gather, Harry went down to the Quayside, though no one knows what he had in mind. It was a snowy night. It seems that when he got to an empty stretch beyond the Baltic Mill there was someone, a woman, there before him, and that this person climbed over the railings and flung herself into the river. Harry hurled a lifebelt after her, to no avail, then ran to the nearest pub to phone for the emergency services. All this I got from the barman, later.

Having made the call, Harry ordered a double and – I think a lot about this – carefully rolled himself a cigarette. He drank the whisky and smoked his tab at leisure until a siren came into earshot, after which he left the building with several other punters and stepped off the pavement, just in time to be mown down by the ambulance.

As you may imagine, I have subjected these pitiful events to lengthy scrutiny. You will understand that I have searched for evidence of order, purpose, irony, comeuppance – in short, for meaning of any kind. I have to tell you that I have made no headway whatever. The bare succeeding facts are these. The woman was never found, despite the sustained efforts of the river police. Anne and Natalie were both safe and well. Harry acquired a plate in his leg and one in his head. He is said to have renounced poetry and moved to Middlesbrough where he occupies himself in some way I have not discovered, minus the company of either woman.

What a hopeless thing a fact can be, a mere dead weight of the actual. But we must work with what we have. People. Their (eventually) obvious sadness. Apparently it must be enough to discover all the merely contingent, wholly unmemorable human *mess* all over again, in papery dribs and drabs like this. Life may not amount to much: it certainly does not amount to literature, to the poems of *Harmonium* and *Les Fleurs du Mal*. Once I would kill for a book. Now I prefer to sit. I do not visit the library often, but when I do I find myself turning the pages of *Practical Photography*, wondering at the terrible unwitting power of the compliant demi-goddesses who lie in wait, there in the smoky light of those badly-imagined bordellos.

I reject this glum diminuendo! Let Harry disappear in style.

I see now that disappointment is a sort of fidelity, that for some people in some places defeat itself can be a virtue if treated with due reverence. Who is to say where disappointment springs from? But we can witness the process of its nurture all about us. The abolition of smoking in the library represents, I see now, what Harry and many others like him knew was bound to happen: not only would their ambitions be unfulfilled, their pleasures would be judged unacceptable. The world – if not Anne, then Natalie, if not her then some other damn thing – the world would be having them. The stupidity of the individual fate would be as irrelevant to this process as to everything else. One day they would look round and discover themselves to be anachronisms in a sense which had little to do with age. As a class, they were to be displaced into the realm of retired facts and foreclosed possibilities. They would take their bitterness with them as a badge of membership, but they would also have the immense, unending satisfaction of having achieved a final unshakeable immobility in which their worst suspicions were both confirmed and celebrated. Harry and his like would achieve their triumphant vindication. They would nod, roll a cigarette, exhale their smoke and vanish from sight. Harry would cease to take up the copy of *Harmonium* or Scarfe's translation of *Les Fleurs du Mal* while the great clock above the library doors unpicked the afternoon stitch by stitch. He would exit, at his own pace, from the library into nowhere, still smoking.

I have not myself smoked for many years, nor written a word till now, but with my task finished and the library at any moment about to close the doors on the world that gave it birth, I feel like lighting up just once more, for the enigmatic hell of it. *Luxe, Calme et Volupte: Tobacconists.*

It Follows Therefore

For Pete Bennet

Thomas Greenwell Bendick was, it proved, the final member of a line of Northumbrian poet-priests which dated back to Elizabethan times. Before Thomas they had produced a minor Elizabethan, a minor Metaphysical, a minor Restoration poet and a minor Romantic – all competent artists necessary to the conduct of literary history but not to the memory of the general reader. The last of the Bendicks, Thomas, flourished in the later reign of Queen Victoria. Thomas was a bachelor who lived with his spinster sister, Mary, serving a parish on the leafy northern outskirts of Newcastle-upon-Tyne.

As well as concerning himself with the souls of his flock, Thomas Bendick wrote his own verses, two collections of which appeared to modest acclaim in his lifetime; and laboured steadily on the writing of a family history, which, though it was never published, may be read on application to the appropriate authority at the library where we meet this evening – as also may his journals, of which more later.

To return to Thomas's ancestry: the first poet-Bendick, Miles, was, it seems, accused of recusancy by agents of Queen Elizabeth I. This not altogether happy state of affairs was compounded by Miles's acquaintance with the notorious Dr John Dee, the famed magician of the time, from whom, it appears, Miles acquired a scrying-glass and other instruments of the occluded arts practised by those who would traffic with the denizens of the nether world. His descendant records an entry from Miles's journal of the time (a journal, I am sorry to say, of which no trace now exists):

15th October. *I shall not admit him though he beat on the door like thunder. Go ye hence, I told him, and trouble me no more. To forestall him I have laid sweet waters and leaves where the circle was sketched. I am in God's care. All's safe. And yet am sore afraid.*

What, we wonder, might Miles have awoken, that was so keen and urgent to enter his dwelling-place? Thomas himself reflects on the unwisdom of any such 'profane arts' before going on to record one of Miles's later entries:

All Souls. *He that is in may not be put out, says the visitor, seated as in a glass and as he were a welcome guest across my table. The nose is missing from his face. His voice is like a gust beneath the barred door. It may be Jesu I am lost. By your grace let me not be lost I pray you. I am in God's hands, am I not?*

This may have been so, but a week later Miles was dead, washed up on the banks of the Tyne and, according to unnamed contemporary witnesses, '*with that look on him as one who sees what angels should not*'.

Thomas, in his own journal, recorded that, to be living in the very house where such events were supposed to have taken place, lent a certain literary *frisson* to his winter evenings. His poems of the period may be felt to reflect this, for example in this gnomic fragment:

> *The secret time has kept,*
> *The empty mystery that is*
> *No mystery, except*

Thomas the Victorian's own ministry was, for its period, theologically orthodox yet liberal in its attitudes. He subscribed generously to a home for fallen girls in the city, and took an interest in its residents, seeking to place them in appropriate employment. At one point he seems to have sought to offer one of these unfortunate creatures – a nineteen year-old called Jane Banks - a place in his own household, but his journal indicates that he acceded, not without regret, to the understandable objections of his sister, who kept house for him. It would not do, clearly.

Little is definitely known of Robert, the seventeenth century Metaphysical poet, although popular tradition identifies him with the protagonist of the folk ballad 'Bobby Bendick's Ride', where the eponymous Bobby flees on horseback across the Wild Hills O'Wanney in Northumberland from an unnamed but evidently malign pursuer. Next came Francis, a contemporary and sometime friend of the great poet-rake Rochester. Francis professed atheism in his verses and quit his living, before fleeing to Rome, there to die in a paupers' hospital while seeking to be admitted to the Roman church. Nearest in time to our own Thomas was Simon, who, like Francis – are you keeping track? – succumbed to the magnetism of the Italianate and sought leave of his bishop to spend an extended period writing and studying in Venice, where he expired during the Carnival of 1825, perhaps of typhus, and is buried in the foreigners' plot on the cemetery-island of San Michele, close by such later arrivals as Stravinsky and Ezra Pound.

All this made for an interesting if not a happy family, distinguished rather for eccentricity than priestly steadiness, but it need not surprise us if Thomas found his ancestors worthy of literary record. His own life had until then offered no comparable excitements. He travelled little, was in religious matters uncontroversial to the point of anonymity, and at the age of forty had no family but for his sister, nor any prospect of one. A man cannot always be writing verses, nor praying neither. Of a winter's night, his work done, he can be understood if he must needs look into things.

The first trace of unease comes in an entry on Thomas's journal from October 1891.

Tuesday evening. It is scarcely worth recording but as I walked in the churchyard towards dusk I found myself uneasy at the leaves from the chestnuts and ashes, blown down in great piles now, arranging themselves endlessly, in the breeze's slightest breath - on the flagged path up to the church porch. Dunbar the sexton and his boy can hardly rake them away quickly enough. I dislike – it is absurd – the possibility that such a drift of leaves might take on the appearance of – what? - of a picture of something, though I know not what. I will take a tincture in hopes of sleeping better. How homely the train to Edinburgh sounds, shuffling by in the dark. Mary says Dunbar should bend his back. Still uneasy when I took up my history to write in it again this evening.

A few days later the problem recurs in another form:

Evening. I had hoped to work on my poems this afternoon but found myself curiously obstructed. I can only compare my situation with that of Mr Dick in **David Copperfield**, *whose epic poem is continually frustrated by the intrusion of King Charles's severed head. In my case I could not even put a name to what it was that wanted to be in the poem. Thus these un-meaning lines:*

> *The secret time has kept,*
> *The empty mystery that is*
> *No mystery, except*

At one point – this is not in itself unusual – I found I had left my desk and was staring out at the lawn and over the low wall into the churchyard. It was the leaves again, forming and reforming themselves in the wind, as though about to arrive at something. Could not look. Went in to Mary, drank tea and spoke with her and a lady visitor. Some malaise of overwork or tedium. Took a little brandy and left the history aside tonight. It will still be there tomorrow. I love to hear the train approach from Newcastle.

There was to be no respite for poor Thomas, though. Three

days later:

All I can write is this foolish fragment, but it is not I who writes it, over and over on the page:

> *The secret time has kept,*
> *The empty mystery that is*
> *No mystery, except*
> *What shall be here betimes,*
> *That has not slept*

To whom can I speak of this? The Bishop is too practical by half. Mary would ascribe this affliction to my indulgence in poetry. I see her growing older and wish she might have married, but this is idle. There seems to be no end of leaves.

And again, the next day:

I have prayed an hour tonight. I went out to confront the leaves where they lay for a little in the angle of two walls in the garden. As I thought, they had settled into a face like one out of Arcimboldo's paintings.

 As I stood there looking, the expression shifted, the mouth opened as though readying to speak and the vile wreath seemed to sit up as one, as though on unseen elbows. There was anger in its look. I turned away in simple terror and walked back to the scullery door, knowing that at any time this thing *might touch me on the shoulder. I was breathless, and cold with perspiration, by the time I reached the hallway. I climbed to the attic and looked down. The wreath stood there below, as though supported on the air. And as I looked, it tilted back to look at me, and then began steadily to ascend, as though the air itself were a staircase, all the while furiously holding my gaze. It reached the window where I watched and when it seemed to press against the glass I thought I must faint dead away, or worse,* open the window to admit it. *The wreath could read my thoughts, for without any lessening of its furious hostility, it smiled widely, and*

31

this for some reason showed me what I had not seen before, that while its face of leaves was utterly convincing in detail, the nose was entirely absent. This made the thing far worse. What I would have done I do not know, but just then a great gust swept against the side of the house, and the wreath disassembled itself on the instant. I ran down to my room and drew the curtains and lit the fire the housemaid had set in the grate. Surely there was no means of entry now. Seeing, and knowing: these were the keys of the case, I reasoned. There was nothing to see. I stood up from lighting the fire and saw myself in the mirror. Immediately I knew I must not look, but man was ever bedevilled by the urgent need of knowing. My face in the mirror was leaves, a great — and somehow wet — gap where the nose should have been. Oh I am lost!

The following day comes the final entry.

Work must be my salvation. I wrote the week's sermon and went through the accounts with Mary, pooh-poohing her anxious enquiries about my well-being. I wrote a number of letters and gave Dunbar instructions. He set to work to burn the leaves. I took out my will and read it over, satisfied. My treasure is not of this world, but Mary shall have what there is. I added an instruction, that my manuscript of family history should be burnt unread, since clearly it could convey no benefit to the reader, though I admit to regret for the loss of my labours. And then I set to write.

Words would not come. Not words of mine. I know that greatness was not my portion as poet, but I had hoped for modest honour. This, it seems, is not to be. When I looked down I found that baffling verse again, written three times over:

> *The secret time has kept,*
> *The empty mystery that is*
> *No mystery, except*
> *What shall be here betimes,*
> *That has not slept*

I struck the verses out, but then the pen insisted and set down baldly:

I care not who you think you are. One will serve as well as any other betimes.

I went up to the mirror once more. I am the Green Man now in autumn's rotten splendour, glaring, fleering, full of greedy loathing, the black wet gap where the nose should be. It is all up with me. Forgive me, Lord.

Dunbar encountered the Reverend Bendick at dusk. He was rushing across the churchyard to the gate by the railway line. The gardener said that Bendick seemed not himself, but frantic and troubled. On the bridle path that runs between the wild plantation and the railway line, Dunbar's boy claimed to have seen something stranger, though the light was poor by then – a running figure in clerical black, raging and screaming in no language the boy could understand, and seeming to have burning leaves falling from the cuffs of his jacket and also, the boy unwillingly revealed, no face, no head even, but as it were a burning stack of leaves, with a hole where the nose should be. The figure flung itself up the steps of the footbridge, and then leapt over the parapet and into the path of the oncoming express train to Edinburgh.

These lurid accounts – that of Dunbar's boy in particular – would have been treated with entire and understandable scepticism, had it not been for the fact that the body of the Reverend Robert Bendick was never recovered. All that lay on the line were leaves, and as Dunbar was heard to remark, he for one was glad not to have the task of gathering them for burning.

The Custodian

I am a harmless drudge of the kind Dr Johnson described in his *Dictionary*; not in fact a lexicographer like the great man himself, but a toiler on the lower slopes of literature and scholarship; an unearther of facts; a provider of notes and a raiser of queries; a pedant with a heart of buckram. At twenty-one I wrote poetry; at thirty-five I quibbled.

You will hear from people like me occasionally in the pages of the *Times Literary Supplement*, putting a professor right on some nearly invisible but – of course - fundamental detail. My representative will be sitting at the back of the conference hall, an unaffiliated scholar, demure but implacable, raising an especially knotty textual point at the time of the afternoon when everyone secretly wants to go home and read a detective story. I held no post, no Fellowship, but none doubted my right to the argument: who else would have taken such recondite matters to heart in that lost world where institutions were few and scholarship was still at least in part the province of the modest gentleman?

My point is this: knowing what I know, after all these years chained to the library, how would I sum myself up? Well, I would say that I am interested in the possession of literature, and in libraries; or, more simply, in possession.

I remember as if it were yesterday the morning I came out of the rain and fog of the late 1940s, up the steps of the library as usual, pausing to watch a tradesman painting a new name at the bottom of the list of Presidents of the Library. Eldon Wooler had died at eighty; the King was dead; he was to be replaced in the year of our lord 1949 by Derwent Rookhope: long live the Priest-King of the ancient library. The rule of the lawyers continued. Of this I say nothing except that I could never have been President, lacking the feral political talents required even in that narrowly specialised sphere. I was merely a reader; a taker of notes; a quibbler, as you can hear.

Through the swing doors the library continued as usual – fog under the great domes, shuddering radiators, idlers browsing and smoking among the journals at the round table, the coffee-hatch redolent of the vivifying roast, though short of coffee in those austere times when only cold and virtue were freely available. To work, I thought, and passed through the double doors, and down a further set of broad stone steps, past Marmite-coloured portraits of Victorian worthies and into the specialised gloom of the basement where my papers were, by unstated agreement, permanently set out on a desk in the Silence Room. As I reached the foot of the stairs, Quinn, the caretaker, appeared in the doorway of the washroom, carrying a mop and bucket and smoking a cigarette forbidden down here. Fifty-odd, ten years my senior, the ruined creature nodded at me bitterly, half in challenge. This I ignored, passing through the black doors of the Silence Room and into my kingdom.

The Silence Room, whose name is self-explanatory, is not large, no larger than the front room of a large townhouse in Jesmond. Its floor is the original parquet. It contains a dozen wooden book-stacks, twelve feet high, in two rows divided by a central aisle. The stacks accommodated what might be called the senile elements of the library – local matters of interest to antiquaries like myself and, thank God, to no one else. My speciality was - is - the poetic tradition of the region; here were my sources, here my happiness, the great, ignored work of scholarly synthesis that could never be completed. Around the walls were tall, glass-fronted cases containing vast volumes of county archives – land sales, things of that sort – dating back to the seventeenth century, waiting then, and waiting now, to be transferred to a more suitable location. I am not, as they say, holding my breath. Between the stacks, facing the walls, are small sloping desks for the use of scholars. In twenty years I could not remember seeing anyone else in the room other than Quinn and the implacable silver-haired librarian, Miss Greenwell, separately pursuing their silent ends. Into these I did not enquire. This was the Silence Room. It meant what it said; or rather, what it did not.

At that time my work concerned the manuscript of a strange eighteenth century text called *A Hexhamshire Tragedy*. This – as you may know? No matter - is a recasting of *King Lear* along the banks of the Tyne. In contrast to some other re-writings of Shakespeare, *A Hexhamshire Tragedy* maintains and even intensifies the horrors of the original. Indeed, by the end of Act Five so many corpses fill the stage that it is left to a hitherto non-speaking servant to sum up and bring down the curtain on this charnel-house of family romance. Interesting, no? My task was to compare this full text with another, incomplete version, apparently of similar date, called *A Tragedy of Killingworth*, in order to determine, if possible, which was the earlier work and publish the fact in the relevant journal. It would be stretching a point to claim that either piece, written anachronistically in late Jacobean blank verse, contained much of strictly literary merit; but if questions of value had been my primary interest I would never have entered the Silence Room all those years ago, would I?

As is my habit I worked steadily until one o'clock, then took my sandwiches to St Andrews churchyard on Darn Crook, there to ponder the resemblance of the rear of the premises overlooking the burial ground to the more famous Howff in Dundee, for funerary locations are another of my interests. As I walked back it began to drizzle, and having cleared during the morning the sky lowered itself to the rooftops, there to produce afresh the fog which made the November afternoon of the smoke-fuelled earlier twentieth century so satisfyingly resemble the Victorian evening beloved of the painter Atkinson Grimshaw – also one of my subjects, I might add. On my return, the library was almost deserted.

As before, Quinn was malingering with a cigarette on the basement steps, directing at me a gaze of hopeless insolence. With a light heart I resumed my work.

When next I looked at my watch it was gone five o'clock. For a moment I could not think what had prompted me to break off from reading. Then it seemed to me that I remembered the sound of a page being turned – swiftly, impatiently turned. But there was no one else in the room. There almost never was. I listened. Nothing. Once more I bent my head to my task.

At six o'clock I heard St Nicholas's bells sounding for Evensong. And it seemed to me that just a moment before the bells began I had heard that abrupt sound again, of paper almost being torn, in impatience or haste. But the room still seemed full of its habitual centenarian silence. I worked on.

At half past seven Quinn knocked on the door of the Silence Room. Time to lock up. I put what I needed in my briefcase, donned my overcoat and then, for no good reason I could discover, walked slowly down the aisles between the stacks, each in succession. All was as it should be in the autumn evening murk.

That night my concentration was poor. At ten I abandoned work and went to bed. But my re-reading of Gibbon held no charms. I lay awake for some time and after that my sleep was fitful.

Normally my dreams are those of an administrator: in the city of dreams some small element of order needs to be restored; this accomplished, all shall be well. That night, however, I dreamed of a library. Not *the* library; though resembling it in many ways – the dome, the stairs to the basement, the caretaker's mop and bucket – but at the same time far larger, with archways leading to additional galleries, with spiral staircases ascending dizzyingly through the domes themselves, it seemed. It was silent and gas-lamps burned silently there and there was a terrible atmosphere, an atmosphere of anticipation both dampened and sharpened, as if what was to happen could not happen until eternity had ended, but would certainly happen then. I had begun with disguised haste to make my way towards the exit when I woke up with a dry mouth. Until dawn I watched the clock and listened to the church bells across the city.

Quinn the caretaker's range of expression was not wide. It encompassed loathing, insubordination and a sense of unjust affliction. The next day as he shuffled to time from his cubby-hole near the washroom I could swear he looked at me with peculiar interest, like a man caught up in watching a horse-race. That morning it took an effort to enter the Silence Room and begin work; and before I began I once more patrolled the stacks.

You will not be surprised to hear that *A Hexhamshire Tragedy* had lost some of its power to compel. Since my Oxford days I had despised those – those many – who in a library cannot settle to their tasks but are endlessly up and down, distracted and distracting, even daring to seek the conversation of the occupied. Had I not been alone I might have done the same. But I struggled on until the lunch hour, when against my habit and inclination I went to the Tyneside Coffee Rooms, realising as I set over my spendthrift's bowl of soup (my sandwiches untouched in their greaseproof paper in my briefcase) that I was there in order to hear the voices of other people. I needed to float, if not to swim, in the warm tide of inane chatter with which all but the nth part of humanity occupies its unreflective leisure. In equal parts shame and terror I dragged my feet down Grey Street and Pudding Chare, back to the library, to the Silence Room. It seemed to be growing dusk already as I passed the raucous printers' bar near the newspaper office.

Work proceeded in a travesty of normality through the afternoon. Nothing untoward occurred. At six o'clock I was tempted to finish early. I listened to St. Nicholas's bells and instructed myself to remain. The bells ceased. I looked down at my notes. Behind me a page turned.

I sprang up in terror to confront – to confront a spry white-haired man in an old-fashioned black suit, standing less than a yard away. He was aged perhaps seventy but in full health. His blue eyes regarded me brightly. A black bow tie and startlingly white shirt completed his attire. In his hands he held a slim black book the size of a volume of poems.

'Good evening,' he said, with a slight unplaceable accent. 'I take it I have the honour of meeting Leonard Dyas.'

'You have the advantage of me, sir,' I said, more calmly then I felt.

'My name is Reinhard Immerich, late of Nuremberg. Delighted to make your acquaintance at long last.'

'I must ask: why would you wish to do that?'

'That will require a little explanation. But now, my friend, I have found you. And you have found me.'

Summoning some self-possession, I replied, 'I was not looking, Mr-'

'Doktor –'

'I wasn't looking, Doktor Immerich.'

'No? Who can say what we do in secret, in secret even from ourselves?'

'Are you a maker of riddles?' I asked, annoyance mixed with unease.

'Like yourself, I aspired to be a maker of sense.'

'I do not think you are a member here. How did you gain entry?'

'I am a reader like you. Libraries are my home.'

'Nevertheless –'

'Nevertheless,' – he put a white hand on my arm, his eyes brightening and seeming to dilate a little - 'nevertheless there are matters of mutual concern requiring urgent attention.' He saw my doubt and anger and said, 'I shall explain, in the proper order. We have a little time. Please, sit.'

To be honest, I needed to sit. My strange companion remained standing close at hand, attentive as a waiter or an executioner. He might have been older than seventy, I thought, but he was wiry and vigorous. As he gazed unblinkingly at me, I felt a migraine about to begin. Soon the first tiny interference, the first spectra, would appear minutely in the corner of my eye, growing from there to consume the whole of my consciousness in a roar of pain.

'This book,' he said, 'is what you have been searching for.'

'I beg your pardon?'

'Take it.'

'But what is it called?'

'Ah, if we knew that.' He placed a white hand on my arm. The spectra swarmed across his face. I looked down. They swarmed across the floor.

'Is this a game?' I asked, struggling to keep my eyes open. Nausea would follow. I needed to lie down.

'You do not want the book? Very well.' He grimaced sadly and made to turn away.

'Wait. I don't understand.'

'Then take the book.' He held it out again.

I must have lost a second or two. Now the book was in my hands, slightly heavy for its size. I turned it over and made to open it, though in my condition heaven knows what I expected to see inside it.

'Not here,' he said, laying the white hand on the cover. 'Save it for the privacy of your apartment.'

'There are questions —' I began.

Quinn knocked heavily on the door.

'And now you must leave,' said Immerich. He helped me up and guided me towards the door.

'What about you?' I said.

Then I was standing outside, blinking as the migraine diminished. Quinn stood waiting. If he had heard me talking he gave no indication.

'Last as usual, Mr Dyas,' he said.

'Of course, Quinn. If I were not, the world would fall from its orbit.'

He smirked, rattled his keys – as if *he* owned the place – and gestured me up the stairs. Of Immerich there was no sign.

At home I placed the book on my desk and then made myself prepare supper and eat it while listening to the news on the wireless. Not until I had washed up did I allow myself back into the study, where I examined the book under a powerful lamp without as yet opening it. The book was, as I thought, oddly heavy. It was odourless and its black binding was hide of some sort I could not identify. I noted these points in my journal and then at length opened the book. On the title page was printed in plain black type **The Book**. There was no author's name nor publishing details nor date on the verso. Beyond that there was nothing at all but a bank of creamy blank pages – in which it was very tempting to begin to write, if one could have mustered anything memorable to say. I closed the book and set it aside again. It lay on the edge of the lamplight, reflecting nothing and admitting less. This was clearly a practical joke of an especially elaborate kind. Quinn was the obvious candidate, though the sophistication of the game made him a doubtful conspirator. I was forced to admire the trick, even as I decided to get to the bottom of the matter.

Then I opened the book again and turned past the title page, noticing as I did so that the act of turning the pages, though I performed it delicately, produced a disproportionately loud sound, like tearing. Before I could consider this, print appeared on the page before me. I blinked; this might be an effect of the now-vanished migraine. But the print remained on the page, and as I began to read I knew with a sudden punch to the heart that before me lay a poem, by Baudelaire, a sonnet: moreover, I knew with exultant certainty that I was the first, the only person, other than the author, ever to have read it. Without letting go of the book I reached across the desk for a sheet of paper and a pencil in order to copy out the text. But when I looked back the sonnet was disappearing line by line, from the bottom upwards. When I turned over the next page was blank. When I turned back, so was the first. I dropped the book. It closed, gently.

I felt forcibly that here was something unnatural and vile. I resisted the urge to fling the book across the room or into the fire, or to wash my hands. I poured a drink, went to the mantelpiece and examined the book from afar in the mirror. Nothing happened, of course. When I returned to the desk I found I could not remember a single word of the poem. Not that I supposed it to exist, as I intended to prove by further examination of the book.

I opened it again at random. The page was blank. But then there was another poem, this time indisputably by W.B. Yeats, late work known only to me, the black type testifying that it had always been there, though I knew that I alone had seen it. Once more I made to copy the poem; once more the words wriggled their way intolerably off the page, out of the world and out of my memory. Though shaken, I resolved on a third and final attempt. Again the blank appeared, and then, again, in a moment or two the immortal type – but this time… this time the poem was mine, the great lyric was mine, whispering its musical secret to the desert air!

And if it was mine, how could I lose? Goodbye to *A Hexhamshire Tragedy* and all the other dryasdust trash of the ages: the world lay all before the poet Dyas! I took up the pencil. Once more the words began to slip away. I cried out in pain. The very act of trying to record the words seemed to accelerate their departure. All gone. If this was my poem, though, then I would remember. But I did not remember – not a line, not a word, not a letter, not the shape of the incomparable rhythms sketched on the inner ear. All I could remember was the fact of forgetting. It was as if I had died. As I sat there my migraine came again and blinded me.

I must have undressed in a trance, since I found myself in bed when I woke to crisp winter sunlight. Even as the year dies, the city is at its most heartening on such a day: frost in the lungs holds out the promise of immortality.

Quinn greeted me sullenly as he unlocked the street entrance and as I passed through the main library the issue desk was still dark. I switched on the lights to the basement stairs and went down. At the bottom I reached out towards the door of the Silence Room, then paused to look round at the dingy hallway and its third-rate paintings before going in. I could hear a tap – still unrepaired – running in the washroom. I opened the door.

'You are mercifully prompt,' said Immerich, attired as before in black, though seeming a little anxious and weary.

'Take your book,' I said, thrusting it at him.

'You will need it, my friend,' he said, with his little bright-eyed smile. 'As you will discover. There is little time. Take my arm, please.' He led me into a far a corner of the room. My confusion was compounded by the sight of a wrought-iron spiral staircase going down through the floor.

'But this – does not exist,' I said.

'You must go first,' said Immerich, placing that vile white hand on my arm. My will, it seemed, was not my own; or it worked secretly. You must decide. We descended perhaps two dozen steps in a shaft in the black dark, Immerich's hand now on my shoulder. At the foot of the steps stood a door, leather-covered, slightly ajar.

'Enter,' breathed Immerich. I pushed the door open.

It was, impossibly, the library. Yet it was not, as a second glance revealed. It was the library magnified – the central gold-blue dome dizzyingly far aloft, the atrium countless storeys high, through which spiral staircases swarmed spiderlike as though in the moment of a dreadful mechanical genesis.

44

Sconces burned on the vast pillars. Arches led off in every direction to further hinted galleries which I knew would be as vast as this, each with its array of further exits. Everything I needed was here.

'Exactly,' said Immerich.

I turned to face him. The door through which we had come had vanished. A thrill of panic ran up my spine and into my brain.

'What is this place?'

'This is the library, of course,' he replied. A wave of pain, then a wave of relief, passed over his face. 'This is what you have been looking for always.'

'I have?'

'Soon you will know it, Mr Dyas.'

'But how do I get out?'

'That is the question,' he said. 'It depends on you. Can you return to the world? Or not? There is no one to find you. Can you open the door again? Or do you seek immortal solitude among these empty halls?' Once again my head flooded with terror; once again my migraine hinted itself. I looked at Immerich as the spectra swam over his face and the shelves behind him. There was a great question I could ask, if only I could frame it. My tongue was thick in my mouth. As I struggled I saw Immerich beginning, as it were, to fade, his jacket-cuffs fraying into dust, his hands shrinking, his white, bright-eyed face seeming to fold in on itself and the shelves appearing flickeringly through his ragged outline. 'Ah, my friend,' he said, in a rusty croak, 'it is true what *The Book of Ecclesiastes* says: "Vanity, all is vanity. Of the making of many books there is no end."' And he was gone, a swirl of dust-motes that glittered in the absent sun.

I awoke in a chair at a nearby desk, awoke to the prospect of eternal solitude, of terror with neither object nor cause, save for the intolerable fact of consciousness itself. The horror of this place was its perfection – and its perfect silence. For days I wandered without hunger or thirst, browsing the texts of my doom. What did I discover? That in the library there was nothing left to aspire to. There was no work so grand, no iconoclasm so startling, no tradition so secure, no ingenuity so trivial that it was not already somewhere to be found in this, the immutable and unreadable temple of perfection – the imaginary museum made over into print and paper.

Even desperation has it habits. To read was a sort of distraction, though without sleep my reading and notemaking soon turned into a delirium of precision, out of which the name of a project soon – in fifty years, you say? – whispered itself to me like evil. Should I read wisely, then perhaps I could discover – you are ahead of me perhaps – my successor, yes, the next true resident of these accursed galleries and catalogues. It is too late, my friend. Too late to leave, too late now to regain the fallen vulgar world. You took the book and read in it. And see, the door by which we entered is now vanished. All that remains for me is to vanish too, released into blessed extinction, and for you to set about your work, custodian of this, the greatest library of all. Farewell, custodian, farewell.

Three Fevers

You find them near the exit doors of libraries. This is a case in point: an oilcloth-covered table with an apologetic scattering of unwanted books seeking places in which to end their days, though in all likelihood their days are already done. This is where we all go, eventually, you might think, whether writers or not – into the void of disregard, beneath time's indifferent gaze (though at some point even the clock overhead will be unceremoniously taken down and dumped in a skip, with its innards hanging out like a cartoon). All those lives' works, remaindered and worse than remaindered, here. The novels that seemed most likely to last; the unreadable thrillers of a decade ago; the groundbreaking studies; the touching/exciting/remarkable/refreshing debuts. This idle paragraph too is subject to the law: in which case better print it somewhere first, give it the ghost of a half-life at least.

★

Three Fevers. Leo Walmlsey. Red Penguin. Price – . Published –. Rusty with salt. On the windowsill of the holiday house in 197-. Along with Ngaio Marsh and Josephine Tey, with *Rogue Male*, *Casino Royale*, *Precious Bane*, *Frenchman's Creek* and *Cautionary Verses*, *Reader's Digest* and *Lilliput*.

The damp in the hallway has waited all winter to greet you. The morning is overcast and as you near the coast the cloud comes down and turns to sea-roke, so the place is hard to find, one of innumerable turnings off the boggy tops.

★

The drunk at seven o'clock is baffled by your lack of interest. He appeals to your better instincts. His life is what he is trying to convey, first to you and then to your female companion. She plays against contemporary expectations by seeming to require you to do something about this melancholy intruder you want to see the back of but feel guilty about because it *is his life* he is trying to communicate to you with these expansive gestures. His consciousness is by now so edited down that it's all peaks and troughs, exuberance pushed aside by despair, sudden enlightenment having the door slammed in its face by the knowledge that he's been here before in a hundred incarnations, trying and failing simultaneously to raid the inarticulate and hold the attention of the passing trade.

'Is she your lass?' You say nothing. 'Is she your lass? Is she? I'm just asking a question pal, all right. Is – she – your – lass?' Actually, you don't know whether she is or not, or whether either of you wants her to be, because it's too early to tell. You have to say something. You are sitting too close to the open fire and you want to move, but the drunk is leaning in, swaying, affectionate, tearful, on the brink of fury.

Eventually the woman says, 'Look, we're just having a quiet drink. Leave us alone, OK?

'OK?' the drunk says, significantly, as if his suspicions have been confirmed. With a conspiratorial smile, he nods and looks round for the support of the imaginary companions he meets most evenings around this time. 'OK? Hear that? She's OK. Right y'are, pet. Hey pal –' he jabs you in the arm with his forefinger – 'you wanna look after her, she's a pearl beyond price, a pearl beyond fookin price. A soft voice is a wonderful thing in a woman, although – paradosically – 'Two barmen have come up quietly alongside him now, their hands extended as though to receive a pass from a loose scrum. 'On the other hand she is more bitter than death, yeah?'

'Right, Derek,' says one of the barmen quietly 'let's be having you now. Let's not have any bother.'

'No bother,' says the drunk, affably. 'No bother. Nae fookin bother. Sorry pet.' They drag him away.

★

You pick up the copy of *Three Fevers*. The idea is to contribute something, a few coppers, to the library. It's very simple. Put twenty pence in the tin, put the book in your pocket, move on to the next thing. For the moment you can't remember what the next thing is meant to be.

You look at the clock and remember, with a pang of something that could be guilt, or duty, or desire.

★

She's late. You explore the house a bit, unable to settle. You put the kettle on and notice the holiday smell of gas. The roke stands at the kitchen window, parting a little sometimes to show the sundial on the sodden lawn. It's too early for this. It's too cold for the seaside. You check the radiators. As promised, they're on to warm the place through. The bed feels a bit damp, though. You light the fire laid in the grate. You leaf through the books on the windowsill. Some you've read, some you never will. *Three Fevers* falls into neither category. You go and turn down the counterpane, with a faint sense of disquiet, as if you're presuming. But isn't that why you're here, or part of it anyway? A long way to come otherwise, you think, as you make a cup of tea you don't want, and the dim afternoon tilts towards evening. You leave a note and walk down the hill to the beach. Soon she will be here. This is just the before part.

There is no beach, really. At low tide there are wide plates of rock stretching away under the fog. The place feels like a building site or something damaged, smeared with

49

malevolent black-green weed. You walk gingerly out, far enough to lose sight of the shore, then stop. Waves break in the distance. The whole place, the huge stone socket of the bay, the wintry village with its rags of bunting strung between the two pubs, seems to be waiting. You go on another twelve steps until you see a skin of water rising over a lip of rock.

You go back to the house. Her car is not outside. You think of ringing but that could be awkward and anyway she will be travelling. That is to say, she will already have left. You pick up the copy of *Three Fevers* and walk down to The Ship. In the bar a couple of locals sit in the yellow silence with pints of mild. The lounge is freezing but you want to be on your own. The landlady puts a light on for you.

You take out the book and read the biographical note about the author, then put the book back in your pocket. Seven o'clock. Hard to say whether this amounts to lateness or not. What were you expecting?

You read the local paper from cover to cover and now it is half past seven. You order another pint and some peanuts. The house is nearly visible from the window of the lounge.

★

You put twenty pence in the tin and turn the book over in your hands. You read the biographical note. Leo Walmsley was a famous novelist in his time, up there with Howard Spring and Gerald Du Maurier, but gone now, it seems, as irrevocably as silent film. That was the impression of him you got in the holiday house, in the village. He was a local author there. He was a real presence, like the Grand National or the Boat Race, fundamental, like Captain Webb on a matchbox, like dense mattresses of ambient smoke in documentary films about the North - something unquestionably *there*, as England was *there*; and as she was not.

You do not bring her name to mind. You do not need to.

50

Instead you think of 'The Work of Art in the Era of Mechanical Reproduction.' And you remember having sex in the lee of a wall behind the palm house, suddenly finding yourselves doing it, a bit pissed, amused rather than scared at the idea of being caught. But desperately urgent, as if something was at stake. The heels of her sandals dug into the backs of your knees. It was a muggy night with shreds of fog under the trees in the park. You had a copy of MacNeice's poems in your jacket pocket. It kept banging against you, so you removed it and placed it on a brick. She took the opportunity to put her pants in her shoulderbag before you continued. The night was holding its hot, damp breath as if something was about to happen. With all the chestnut trees it was like being in a candelabra'd ballroom after the event, when the coaches had taken the guests away and the servants could indulge themselves among the leftovers.

You put the copy of *Three Fevers* in your pocket and go to keep your evening's appointment.

★

In the pub you realise your companion has been watching you for some time.

'Sorry, Jan,' you say. 'Something just reminded me. You know.'

'What of?' She smiles sympathetically.

'I don't know.'

'Shall we get off, then?' She is already on her feet.

There is a jazz event you are meant to be going to. You like jazz. You don't mind sitting with the other ageing aficionados in grubby pub concert rooms with only one sort of lager on and no Guinness, even though there are hardly any women in this world. Tonight, though, you feel absolutely exhausted. But it would be death (the death of what?) to pull out now. It's much too late for that kind of complication. You go slowly down towards the quayside, passing the Lit and Phil library where the book manifested itself to you. You wonder if you should mention this, but what exactly is there to mention? You navigate like a sensible, tolerant, grown-up couple past the bellowing herds of stags and the screeching flocks of hens, and all the time you wonder if it's too late to be here now, starting something you perhaps can't finish. What must your companion be thinking? She has, as they say, made an effort.

'I like the way you've had your hair done,' you say. 'And your jacket. Is that new?' She nods. Now it is her turn to be elsewhere.

'Shall we have another drink first?' she asks, stepping off the pavement and into the Crown Posada without waiting for a reply. It is one of the quiet intervals of the evening – unpredictable half hours when you can get a seat before the human wave breaks back up the hill. She leaves you to order and finds a table down at the far end. The choice of position seems ominous. By the hatch, as ever, stands the solitary silver-haired man with the hare lip, drinking one of the dozen pints he soberly gets through on the average night. It is hard to imagine that he has ever had sex. The same could be said of you and your companion. You haven't, of course, not with each other. You think the two of you must look resigned to an awkward accommodation, like bitter pensioners eating their ice creams in an empty matinee cinema while those on screen grind away obliviously. You've seen lots of couples like yourselves in this pub – sort-of couples, maybe couples, clandestine couples, former couples, uneasy pairings just about functioning by means of varying ratios of goodwill and need, like people brought together by rail crashes or wartime bombing, long after the cruel, exciting glamour of the accident has worn away, when the ordinariness stretches ahead for the rest of your lifetimes, without remission. It is a good thing the mirrors on the opposite wall are placed too high for you to see yourselves. You wish you had something to read, apart from *Three Fevers*, which you have not even begun and never will. You know that down in the snug there is a shelf of books, car manuals mainly. You wonder who would spend an evening reading a car manual. Or 'consulting' one. You have not consulted memory: it has simply moved in and occupied the space where once you were.

'Right, what is it?' she says when you sit down with the drinks. You have somehow bought yourself a large vodka as well as a pint.

Your hand has gone to your pocket.

'What have you got there?'

'Sorry?'

'You keep fingering it. What is it?'

'A book.'

'Let's see.'

You hand it to her.

'Never heard of him. Why've you bought this? It's ancient.' She is quizzical but still theoretically friendly. Her comments are probably fatal, though. Is she in fact talking about the book? You drink half your pint in a single swallow.

'Steady,' she says. 'Look. What's wrong?'

★

You could not swear how many pints you've had. At half past nine you rise carefully and leave the still-empty pub, giving the landlady a stately nod which clearly doesn't fool her at all. You go back up the hill, a little breathless and sidelong in the cold. The roke has finally cleared, now that there is nothing to see. The house is dark. The only car is yours. You go into the kitchen, switch on the light and come out again. You bring *Three Fevers* with you and place it on the grass by the sundial's base. In the faint light from the kitchen you struggle to read the inscription around the clockface of the sundial. *My days are as a shadow that declineth.*

'Amen to that,' you announce to the night in general

and set off back downhill to use the phone in the pub. When you ask the landlady for change you find yourself explaining that your friend is late, but clearly she would rather you didn't go into it. Your distress must be evident. You order a large Bell's and stand it on top of the telephone coinbox.

The phone is answered immediately.

'Now then, now then, who's this?' The speaker is clearly drunk. He sounds as if he has been waiting for this moment. A hand brushes over the mouthpiece but you hear a woman laughing in the background, then several voices, all lit up with drink. They're all there, all of them.

'Is Karen there, please?'

More laughter. Muffled exchanges. The receiver put down heavily.

Then someone picks it up.

'Yes?'

'Karen?'

'What do you want?' She sounds irritated.

'I'm here. Where the fuck are you?'

'Where the fuck am I? I should have thought that was obvious.' More laughter. The phone is put down.

Back at the house you manage to light a fire in the kitchen grate. You go out and retrieve *Three Fevers* from the lawn, then kneel by the fire, tear the book up and feed it a few pages at a time into the flames. Even though you're drunk you can sense that this is not really adequate (never mind necessary) in symbolic terms, but that it is also irrevocable. Something has been done forever. You go to sleep on the settee in the garden lounge in the house that comfortably sleeps six.

*

When you get sober you go home and read a lot of books, about twenty years' worth at an average of four a week, and you become approximately as well read as you hoped to be. You never read *Three Fevers* or anything else by Leo Walmsley, though you never forget a name. Once there is an item about him on the regional television news. Someone is attempting to open a museum dedicated to him in the village. This sounds at once understandable and slightly mad, as though everyone should have a museum opened in their names. How could there be enough memoriousness to go round? You and she might have to take on the task of each other's museums. What would you put in hers? A pub telephone, a couple of hotel rooms, a long silence interrupted by laughter on some topic you're not privy to.

You read a good deal of poetry. You must be reading the rations meant for others. You encounter a poem by Douglas Dunn, which imagines a couple waltzing in foggy meadows near the edge of cliffs. You find that without intending to you have committed it to memory. Whenever the poem surfaces, you flinch a little.

★

'Because you do seem very bothered this evening,' your companion says. ' Is it me? Have I done something? Do you want me to go?'

'No,' you say. She stands up. 'Hang on.' She sits down again, perching on the edge of the bench, her jacket and bag still in her folded arms.

'Well?'

You are very tired. You have never been so tired in your life. She looks at her watch and bites her tongue.

'It's about this poem.'

'What, one in that book?'

'No.'

'What poem, then?'

'You know that drunk?'

'What about him?'

'It's like that.'

'What is? Like what? What on earth are you on about?'

'I dunno.'

'Well then.' She stands up again. 'Let's leave it, eh?'

You have no comment to make on this. She leaves. She actually walks out without looking back. You search for your feelings about this, but now you are inert as a sodden log in a canal. No one should aim any expectations your way for a bit. You stock up on vodka, which you never drink normally, and you sit while the pub fills and empties. Anyone looking might see you flinch as the poem rises into your mind again: 'Your hand, and my hand, and your face that I cannot see.'

The Cricket Match
at Green Lock

It was one of the blessedly neglected parts of England, a half-hidden place of ponds and canals where railways met and left for either coast, running between the brick warehouses and absent-minded ditches of slowly-vanishing industries. We hadn't played Green Lock before, nor heard of them, in fact. That year's game was a fixture in the Cup. It was early on that Saturday when we boarded the train at York and went down, too early for the wedding parties, so we had a couple of compartments to ourselves. We sat drowsing or smoking or doing the crossword and reading of Yorkshire's then-habitual triumphs in J.M Kilburn's column in the *Post*.

At Retford we changed to a local stopping train that chugged steadily down alleys of tall, pointed-roofed and strangely narrow houses, then out through hawthorn scrub and into the backlands. This was paradise, it seemed to me, this land of gravel pits and the intricate intersections of dreadnought Victorian bridges spanning canals and slow, soupy rivers where the barges seemed barely to move on those long stretches that reached into strange Midland distances. It was a place of blissful uneventfulness, where a thing – an oiled Surridge bat, a heavy roller - would stay where you left it until worm or rust duly intervened.

We ran once more into woods – birches and aspens - and slowed for Green Lock, emerging blinking from under the station awning in the strong late-morning sunlight. We carried our bags of kit the short distance to the signposted cricket grounds, through the deserted streets, past the yew-shadowed churchyard and the memorial to the Great War with its neatly incised Branstons and Henfreys and Keyworths, men of the long-disbanded Light Infantry. Our footsteps bounced off the walls as we passed through the shadows of their tall quiet houses.

There seemed to be nobody about as we walked up the chalky path. It was just wide enough for a vehicle, though none came. I say 'grounds', for there were apparently several, half-concealed among small dense woodlands beyond the village. Further pools and canals were visible among the trees. We chose the nearest, making for the pavilion, a large and elderly white-painted shed with a broken roof-ridge. It had a damp verandah, and a rain-warped scoreboard leaned unsteadily against one wall, next to a large water-butt fed from a cracked drainpipe.

We trooped in and changed into our whites. Then we waited, smoking and nattering on the verandah, drowsing on deckchairs on the grass, taking spells in the tumbledown nets that seemed half in the woods themselves. And time went by, and nothing happened, which was fine, but after all there was a match to be played.

'So where have the other lot got to?' Bennet asked, looking sceptically into the bowl of his pipe. 'Seems a bit queer. I mean, they're playing at home. Where are the womenfolk? There's lunch to be got.'

'It's a rum do. Might be a walkover,' said Crowe.

Bennet gave him a look. The point was to play. Otherwise why bother?

'Long way to come if we're not going to play,' I said.

'Where's Will?' said Bennet.

'Here, Skipper.' Will emerged from behind the pavilion. He was the youngest, a lad of sixteen and the (generally) uncomplaining twelfth man. He lived with his mother, a widow since Arnhem, where her husband's glider went into a canal. We looked after him, in our way.

'Go to the pub and find out where the Green Lock XI have got to.'

'Do I have to, Skipper?' Beneath his blonde fringe, Will blinked in the heat.

'Yes, Blondie, you have to. Take a bag and bring some bottles of beer back with you. And get yourself a dandelion and burdock. This should cover it. Make sure you bring some change.'

Will sighed, then grinned and set off, disappearing round the end of the pavilion.

'Stop him getting bored,' said Bennet.

'I thought that must be it,' I said. 'What about us?'

'We pass our time in philosophical reflection.'

The heat stood tall, pressing us to the grass or deeper into the deckchairs. In the West high clouds were building, friendly enough as yet, but big, as though marshalling themselves before coming over. Flies droned. Will seemed to have got lost.

'Well bugger this,' said Bennet eventually, getting up and looking around. 'Oh – hang on. Someone coming.' We all looked where he looked. A figure in an umpire's white coat and broad white hat had appeared from the woods by an unseen path and was slowly approaching.

'Morning,' said Bennet.

'I'm afraid you're on the wrong pitch, gentlemen,' said the umpire. He was a thin, grey character, unusual for that date in affecting dark glasses. He also wore a clerical collar. 'If you'd care to follow me.' He turned and set off again. He was perfectly civil but not exactly effusive.

Bennet shrugged. We gathered our kit and followed the by-now vanished umpire. In the hanging shadows of the wood I could happily have lain down to sleep.

After a couple of hundred yards we emerged across a footbridge over a stream, on the edge of a pitch apparently identical to the one we had recently left, right down to the scoreboard and the water-butt. As we approached the pavilion our opponents appeared from the line of woods opposite, strung out at equal intervals, each man moving slowly to take up a place in the field. While we dumped the kit in the pavilion, Bennet went to the middle for the toss.

When we came out onto the verandah he was on his way back.

'Well?'

'We'll bat.'

'I guessed that somehow. Friendly bunch.'

'Very.'

Herbert and Armstrong padded up and went to the middle.

'We're doing the scoreboard as well, are we?' I asked.

'Looks like it,' said Bennet.

'I'm starving,' said Elliot.

'And thirsty,' said Crowe.

'Will should be back with the beer in a minute,' said Bennet.

'If he can find us. Geography isn't his strong suit,' said Crowe.

'Stop complaining,' said Bennet. Armstrong clipped a looseness past fine leg. 'Now we're off the mark.'

Herbert and Armstrong made brisk progress for half an hour against the military medium pace of the Green Lock bowlers. The heat intensified steadily, and there was a tinge of charcoal and slate behind the leading edge of the cloud mass now approaching over the woods. Eventually Armstrong skied one to long leg. It took an age to come down. The Green Lock fielder waited without moving. In defiance of all coaching he only raised his hands at the very last second, but took an effortless catch and returned the ball to the keeper in a single movement. Crowe went in and immediately gave a catch behind, followed by Elliot, who hit a return ball to the bowler. I began to find the mixture of assurance and indifference with which the fielders took their chances slightly eerie. Likewise the absence of applause from their team-mates.

I looked at my watch. Time seemed to be taking its time to pass. Will must have found some other way to amuse himself. He'd be in for it when he got back. The Skipper was not a happy man.

We were a decent club side, occasionally feeding a youngster on to the County Colts. We didn't have to field makeweights or rabbits. We'd been finalists a few years back. More, we were a Yorkshire side, grudging, unyielding, bred to compete for a bent penny as fiercely as for a cup. We knew gamesmanship and would engage in it ourselves if necessary. Against Green Lock, though, we looked like a side of ringers and ancient occasionals scraped together for a Sunday beer match on some stockbrokers' featherbed in Surrey. Stands began and failed to develop. People played out of character. Even Bennet himself, blocker and nudger supreme, was quickly out-played, much to his ill-concealed fury.

Going in at number seven, I was as bad as anyone. But I got some sense of why. By then the spinners were on at both ends and the fielding ring was close in. At 70 for 5 we needed some quick runs. I took guard, then had a look round. The Green Lock fielders were young men but grey with exhaustion, as if they'd been outdoors all winter. To a man they were whippet-thin, dressed in cobbled-up, washed-to-rags kits out of the Ark. But it was the stare that did for me. They all had it, looking at you and through you without recognition or acknowledgement: nothing personal, no particular effort to intimidate, but a level, unblinking gaze of ferocious, pessimistic expectancy, which surely deserved to be focused on some matter graver than cricket. I lasted three balls, spooning a catch to short leg. I walked back through the silence, watching the clouds, great darkening rain-stacks now. They seemed to have halted just beyond the village. There came the faintest rumble of thunder far off, and the birds had fallen quiet.

SEAN O'BRIEN

Two women had appeared, pale, plain, grimly dressed twin sisters in their sixties. They unpacked a picnic basket of grey-looking pies and mousetrap cheese on a trestle table in the pavilion. A large enamelled tea-pot appeared. Then they stood looking out at the pitch without speaking. The heat had tired me unusually and I sat sleepily, slowly taking my pads off, one eye to the game and one eye watching them watching. After a while they turned their heads to look expressionlessly at one another and then looked away again, a moment before Crowe's yeoman heave allowed a long-hop to dismantle his wicket. At lunch we were 78 for 7, and it seemed a very long way to have come for this uncomfortable reception and the humiliation which seemed likely to await us. It was my job to send the scores in to the local paper. Perhaps this time I might just forget.

The team filed in and stood in silence like schoolboys facing a twin-headed matron.

'Lunch, gentlemen,' said one sister. 'Help yourselves.' The pair were putting their coats on.

'What about the Green Lock players? Where are they?' asked Bennet.

'They must fend for themselves, I'm afraid,' said the other sister.

'Have you seen our twelfth man – that fair boy? We've lost him.'

'No boys here,' said the first sister.

In a voice that brooked no further questions, the second added, 'Now you'll excuse us. We'll be back to collect the crockery.' And off they went round the side of the pavilion.

'Is this some elaborate joke?' asked Elliot.

'Bloody creepy, I think,' said Herbert.

'Well,' said Bennet, ever the pragmatist, 'we may as well go on and eat. Shame to let it go to waste.' There was general if muted agreement. We set about the meagre fare with as good an appetite as we could muster.

'What about Will?' asked Herbert.

'His fault if there's none left, the dozy beggar,' said Bennet, loading his plate. 'These pies aren't as bad as they look.'

'Someone should go and look for him,' I said.

'Then someone should get on with it,' Crowe muttered through a mouthful of cheese.' I hope the little bugger hasn't drunk all the ale.'

The weather waited until lunch was done and our cigarettes extinguished. Then the clouds finally closed over the pitch and the rain began – a storm in fact. Vicious lightning came ripping down, with earth-moving thunderclaps and great sheets of water flogged against the earth in blinding succession.

'Looks as if we've got a draw,' said Bennet. 'It could be worse. The other lot don't seem to be coming back, nor the cheerful padre.'

For a time we enjoyed the complacent sensation of being in shelter and able to watch the weather's violence, though the pitch was barely visible, such was the intensity of the storm. Then Elliot pointed out that water was coming up through the floorboards. Even as we looked, it rose to lap at the seams of our boots.

'This is ridiculous,' said Crowe.

'So what do we do?' asked Herbert.

'We bale out,' said Bennet. 'Make for the village and the pub.' A small muddy wave rolled through the door of the pavilion. 'Every man for himself!' The others laughed as they ran out into the deluge.

Burdened with our bags of gear, we struggled over the outfield towards the path back through the woods. Within a few yards we were ankle-deep. The rain fell so heavily we had to stoop. I saw Herbert fall and struggle back to his feet, then saw Elliot ahead of me among the trees in the momentary flare of a lightning-bolt before it blinded me. Blinking and cursing, I staggered over the swimming footbridge above the torrential ditch and then skated off the path into a fern-bed, where I too fell and gave up for a minute, gasping, half-drowned and half-hysterical at the violent absurdity of the situation. The rain slackened for a moment and I struggled back to the path, finding there a trail of abandoned gear. I went blundering on, half-choked. And then a grey-white figure seemed to rise up before me, wielding a cricket bat like a cudgel. My effort to duck was fuddled and too late.

When I awoke, I thought the top of my head had come off. The rain had stopped. The woods steamed in the heat and the birds were singing. Headache aside, I could find no evidence of injury. Stiffly, and not caring to think too much, I made my way through the wood, from which all the dropped gear seemed to have been retrieved, and across the further pitch. The clouds had moved on, leaving the sky a rich midsummer blue. There was no one about as I approached the pavilion.

I heard the sound of running water. Without knowing why, I walked past the verandah to look at where the water-butt stood, a vast pitch-coloured wooden barrel, six feet high, bound with iron hoops. The drainpipe was not even dripping, but water spilled from the rim of the barrel as though violently stirred. Against my will, I found myself approaching and looking down into the water. One of the most terrifying things I had ever witnessed was in the film of *Richard III*, where Clarence, who has unwittingly foreseen his death in a dream, is drowned by the murderers, in a butt of Malmsey wine. The horror of that fate, of that inescapable confinement, and of that knowledge of what must follow – these were all conveyed in the shocked, innocent face of Will as he stared blindly up through the dark waters in the rainbarrel, struggling in despair before he sank entirely from sight.

I found the others in the dim, rather chilly pub, subdued but consoling themselves with pints of Marston's. There were no other customers.

'You took your time,' said Bennet, fiddling with his

pipe.

'Lost my way.'

'It was a bit wet back there,' said Bennet. He held my gaze for a moment. No one else seemed to notice. 'Anyway, hurry up – there's a train out in twenty minutes.' No one, I could tell, was going to say anything about the events in the wood, still less about Will.

I turned to the bar. The grey sisters awaited my order.

'No boys here,' the nearest said, before I could ask.

We never did complete the fixture. Green Lock, we were given to understand, had waited for us on one of the other pitches. Crowe looked to the heavens: trust these southern foreigners. They were expelled from the competition, and then, so I heard, disbanded altogether. We were knocked out by Loftus Seconds, of all people. Then, over the next couple of years, our own team began to break up too. Soon there was no one to run the club, and our beautiful ground in the Hambledon Hills was sold for building. As well build on a graveyard, Bennet said. Perhaps it was just that people grew older, passed on to other interests, acquired responsibilities. A certain zest had gone out of our excursions, just as the steam trains were being withdrawn from service. We became one more insomniac's footnote in the history of club cricket. Without cricket we lost touch with each other. Thus the waters closed over us, as it were. A great age of the larger game was, I now see, likewise coming towards its end, as the pre-eminent Yorkshire side of the day began to lose their powers to the passing years. The world I knew – the world of youth, Saturdays, cricket, steam railways and the great summery eventless counties of England - was passing away. Where could I turn then but to history, in search of the sources of that intoxicating silence and what lay beneath it?

I have spent my life teaching history. Now that life is almost done too, and I know that I have never been quite truthful about the discoveries I made, as it were, in the field.

Will the twelfth man was declared a missing person. His mother was beside herself. Some bright spark – Crowe, possibly – suggested that the boy had run away to join the Army. But we never saw or heard of Will again, though he remained the awful companion of my dreams.

A few years ago, at a loose end, I found myself on board the dismal single-carriage train that nowadays serves parts of that old cross-country line. The odd tall houses still stood, though patches of the woods had been cut down for new estates. Green Lock was now an unmanned halt. The village itself seemed much as I remembered, a still place gone past waiting. There were two anachronistic old men playing dominoes over a pint of mild in the pub, where a bored young slattern with dragged-back peroxided hair condescended to serve me a beer and a sandwich.

Afterwards I walked up past the church and the war memorial and the newish road that ran through the woods towards the cricket pitches. It was hard to find my way in this place forty years later, when so much of this low-lying ground had been developed for housing to exploit the attractions of rivers and canals. I hoped it never rained on the inhabitants of this flood-plain. I hope it did not rain on them as it rained on 'B' company of the Third Battalion of the Light Infantry. The men of 'B' company were holding a stretch of the line among the dykes and locks of the muddy Belgian riverscape in June 1916 against a determined assault by a regiment of Pomeranian Grenadiers. Following the unremitting wetness of the spring that year, a combination of unprecedented rains and artillery damage produced flash floods. Despite the resulting chaos, hand-to-hand fighting continued, and along with numerous German Grenadiers every last man of 'B' company was killed or drowned in the course of an afternoon, including the lock-keepers, rivermen and farm labourers who made up the Green Lock cricket XI.

The weather was dry on the day I returned to Green

Lock, so that when I discovered the remaining cricket pitch, hidden away beyond willows and aspens and edged by near-dry ditches, there was nothing to be afraid of. Nevertheless, even though I had come so far to find the place, I decided not to approach the pavilion or to check whether on its far side stood a water-butt. An hour later I sat on the empty local train, the sports pages open before me unread. They say you can never go back. They might add that you can never escape.

Silvie: A Romance

'Poetic genius is dead, but the genius of suspicion has come into the world.'
Stendhal, *Memoirs of an Egotist*

'As light as love, as ruthless as the Czar'
Douglas Dunn, 'The Swing'

i

I had been looking one dull afternoon into Elliot's energetic versions of Verlaine's erotic poems, which prompted me, for reasons I no longer remember, to check the catalogue and then go up to the gallery in search of a copy of Aretino's notorious *Postures*. Predictably the volume was not to be found there, though the space it had occupied in that sooty, unvisited district of the library was still empty. As I turned away, I caught a glimpse of something pushed to the back of the shelf and partly hidden behind the adjacent volumes. I reached in and removed it. It was an old school exercise book, a *cahier* of a kind I suspect is hardly to be found nowadays. One should of course be surprised neither by what is missing from a library nor what is unofficially added to it: I remember the stern injunction of Dr Larkin, thirty years ago, not to put bacon sandwiches in the books in *his* library. But what I held in my hands was neither a frivolous nor an unwitting addition to the stock. The name on the front page was Stephen Ash, of whom some of you here tonight will certainly have heard. Ash was the *poete maudit* of the city, a great talent squandered on drink, drugs and – to some minds perverse – sensual indulgence, who leapt from the Tyne Bridge ten years ago, aged forty nine, leaving scarcely a handful of fugitive publications and a local reputation as the man destined for greatness who went mysteriously wrong.

Efforts are being made to clarify Ash's achievement, scattered and fragmentary as it must appear, and to assemble definitive texts in order to establish his reputation properly. But minor poets, living or dead, are many, and the attention of even that tiny portion of the world which takes an interest in poetry is difficult to claim. If Stephen Ash requires a myth to bring his name into relief, perhaps the material contained in this little jotter will supply it. I leave it for you to judge, adding only that the handwriting has been expertly authenticated. Whether what you are about to read is a fantastic tale, or a deluded testimony, or a work without a category, you must decide for yourselves, ladies and gentlemen. Here follows the manuscript of *Sylvie*, narrated in the first person.

ii

There is an essay to be written about the eroticism of libraries. Since I am not French, this is not it. But Sylvie was French, and this story is about her, Sylvie, the librarian, the One, though my hopes are long dead.

In those days I spent most of my waking life in the library, claiming a seat at the long table in the toe of the L-shaped gallery, under the clock, in order to work on what I thought would be my first book of poems. I had a few things in magazines, a bit of encouragement here and there. The manuscript is still around, at home somewhere, beyond resurrection. I began it in spring when I should have been writing up my thesis, whose subject was '"To cease upon the midnight with no pain": Attitudes to Mortality in Keats and Beddoes.' Beddoes, not much recalled now, was a minor Romantic poet – author of *Death's Jest-Book*, and a doctor doomed by syphilis. This was of course a young man's perfect subject, death-fixated, full of portent.

But it could not compete with the impulse to write my own poems. Nor, I have come to understand, could it compete with the disquieting influences which were beginning to make themselves felt in the sphere of literary criticism. I mean those continental developments we now call Theory – structuralism, post-structuralism, deconstruction and the rest. All of these threatened and then for a time overwhelmed and transformed the hitherto relatively stable world of English-speaking Lit Crit (I simplify grossly here, of course, for I want to *get on with the story* quite as much as you do), whose attitudes and methods were instinctively empirical, commonsensical and moralistic. Theory destabilised the text, abolished the author and made of the theorist an infinitely sceptical philosopher-king for whom morality was a construct like any other. From now on, literature would serve the theorist. You see?... I told myself I was taking a break from my academic work to digest the implications of Theory, but in fact I had given my commitment wholly to writing poems.

I decided to stay in town for the summer instead of travelling. By July all my friends had gone. All the better to concentrate. My head cleared after the smoky indulgence of the winter in the various freezing flats of my companions of those days. As soon as Quinn the caretaker opened the doors, and before Mrs Bolam had set her ancient coffee-urn to boil, I was in my seat and beginning work. There is nothing better than work. It is better than love, than sex, than money or success. Work taketh away care. Or usually it does.

What I speak of took place long ago, at the dope-hazed, patchouli-scented start of the Seventies, that retarded interregnum when it seemed that one world had finished before it had properly begun, while the next was yet to be born. A modest self-absorption and plenty of Afghan black seemed the wisest course, by which I mean the most obvious, the easiest.

So I can barely remember a line of my poetry of that time – it was not what I thought it was - and nothing of my thesis. But I remember Sylvie. I went to the issue desk to have a book brought up from the store, and there she was, turning to face me, like the young blonde Catherine Deneuve, in a short, strappy black summer dress like the one the actress had worn when introduced to the London press a few years previously. Not quite the librarians' usual attire. Sylvie had a cat's considering green eyes.

'I don't think we've met,' I said.

She smiled, then nodded with charming formality.

'No. I am Sylvie. And you –' – here she gave a heart-stopping moue, indicative of thought, and placed a finger to her lips. 'Ah – you are Doctor Ash.' What was that perfume?

'Not a doctor, I'm afraid. Not yet. Probably never.' Not the heavy musk the local girls went in for in their kohl-rimmed torpor. This was something austere, stylish, worn on the air like a single unbroken line of blue pencil. I wanted to pick her up and breathe her.

'Never? But that is sad.' If Sylvie thought it was sad, then that was wonderful. Let me be sad. I had the strange sensation of being about to step off and up into the air.

'Dr – Mr Ash?' I shook myself. Sylvie wore a half-smile. 'Go and sit down. I will have this book brought to you.' I was sure the entire staff was hers to command. I returned to my seat with Sylvie's perfume in my head like not-quite-audible music, a Debussy tone-poem where the orchestra fell, with impeccable élan, off a cliff and into the coal-mine depths of outer space.

A voice awoke me.

'You were asking for this, Mr Ash?' Miss Greenwell, the implacable silver-haired librarian, was holding a copy of Sade's *Justine*. I seemed unable to speak. 'Because normally there has to be a member of the clergy present,' Miss Greenwell continued.

'It's a mistake,' I said. I had gone crimson.

'And you have to keep your hands on the table while you read it. Normally.' Miss Greenwell's facial expression varied between the stern and the inscrutable.

'This isn't what I requested.'

'Really? Is this your handwriting?' She handed me the order slip.

It was, indisputably, my handwriting.

'I asked for Stendhal's *Memoirs of an Egotist.*'

'Did you now?'

'Honestly, Miss Greenwell.' I felt about fourteen.

'It's easy to allow yourself to be distracted, Mr Ash, isn't it? With the hot weather and so on. Will you still be requiring the Stendhal?'

'Yes, please.'

'I'll see to it, then. Would you like a glass of water, Mr Ash?' She tilted her head and I followed her gaze down to my sheet of notes on the tabletop. There were only about fifty copies of Sylvie's name there. 'Perhaps you should get some fresh air.' She disappeared around the corner and I heard faint female laughter. Miss Greenwell too had surrendered to the presence of Sylvie.

It was Sylvie who brought the Stendhal.

'You like this? *Memoirs of an Egoist*? His title is correct. He speaks for all men in that way, perhaps.'

'De Sade was no better. *Justine?* I didn't know they had it here.'

'In the librarian's special case.'

'Have you read it?' I asked. She did not reply. 'And how did you do that?'

'I am sorry?'

'Whatever you did with the request slip.'

Sylvie laughed.

'Miss Greenwell is very fierce, no? She could be scary.'

Despite myself, I smiled. Sylvie smiled back. I was glad I was sitting down; otherwise I would have had to lie on the floor to contemplate the fact that I was going to live forever, with Sylvie.

'You're not going to tell me, are you? Why did you do it?'

She smiled me to death and back.

'You should get on with your work. And so must I, Mr–not–Dr Ash.' She clapped her hands. 'So.'

'Will you have lunch with me?'

'Impossible, Mr Ash.'

'It's Stephen,' I said, but she was gone.

The other staff were greatly amused by the courtship. Sylvie had become an immediate favourite with them. She brought summer into the dim interior. It took me a week of persuasion – carefully observed, with much whispered comment, during which I got no work done - before she agreed that yes, she would come for lunch, 'for a little while.'

But I could hardly ask her to the ruins of my flat. And what did she eat? And she was French, and so where on earth could I take her? It would have to be Wicksteeds. I put on my jacket and tie and went to meet her at Monument. Her lateness was as nothing to the beautiful simplicity of her air-blue dress. Wicksteeds' fashion department retired into monochrome around her and in the restaurant the munching wifies exchanged glances of admiring resignation. But what would Sylvie eat?

Almost nothing. A spoonful of soup, a scrap of bread, an apple she cut into perfect eighths.

'Stop staring, Stephen, please. It's rude.' She giggled at me.

'I can't help it.'

'You must discipline yourself.'

'Yes. Where are you from? Did you go to university?

Why are you here?'

'Are you a policeman? Are you a spy? Or a gaoler, perhaps?'

'I'm sorry, Sylvie.' When I reached for her hand, she graciously withdrew it as though conferring a gift.

'You rush, rush, rush. Eat your food. Yes?'

Sylvie was Sylvie Scarron. She was Parisian, had studied English and Philosophy (ah) at one of the Paris universities but had decided scholarship was not for her – though she seemed to have read everything – and then trained as a librarian and wanted to travel. And had no family but an aged aunt, Hortense, a nun in a closed order. Sylvie's earthly solitude only made her more desirable, but I found my enquiries deflected. What about me? Oh, all about me. More than anyone, even a lover, could have wanted to know about *me*, some of it distinctly speculative, such as how my poems would develop and how at some time I would work in the United States. She absorbed it all with no glimmer of boredom. The restaurant emptied.

'Now I must go,' she said.

'Let me see you home. Where is that?'

'I am not going home.'

'Then where?'

She smiled.

'That is not your business. Stephen. Walk me to Haymarket, please.'

I did as commanded. We parted outside the old hotel. She would see me in the library and agreed to think about another date. 'That is what you call it – a date?' She smiled and set off towards the university. The street stood back to admire her.

And then I followed her, with what I imagined was discretion, through the arch, past the gallery, along the flowering precinct and out opposite the hospital – where a crimson slingbacked Citroen, elderly but well-maintained, was waiting. As Sylvie approached, a man got out and gave a questioning nod. He was tall and shaven-headed and wore small sunglasses like goggles. Despite the heat he had a leather jacket. In response Sylvie spread her arms in an exuberant shrug. He nodded again without expression and they drove off.

The weekend passed in infuriated, workless tedium.

So I had a rival. Was he a rival? A brother? She had no family. A friend? Girls like Sylvie can't have friends, I thought. What man would settle for friendship? Perhaps I might have to. The prospect of that pain was unthinkable. My rival seemed older, though it was hard to tell.

Worse, there was no way to raise the matter without revealing that I had followed her. So I sulked. I went to the library and sulked as conspicuously as possible. I was offhand, absent, sullen. Sylvie appeared, or affected, not to notice. She gave out happiness to the library's other users as easily as she issued books or responded to enquiries. Beneath the clock, I raged. Eventually I approached the issue desk.

'Something is troubling you, Stephen.'

'Not really.'

'As you wish. Would you excuse me?'

She came past and began to place some books on the return shelves.

'So would you come out with me again?' I blurted. 'It's just –'

'Of course. But you are so worried about asking this simple thing. Really, Stephen.' She stroked my hand. 'Let us say that when this place closes on Wednesday you can take me to a bar.'

In the rest of the day I made a certain amount of progress with my work, though it was taking on an unexpectedly erotic cast, which made me conceal the manuscript in my briefcase when I went for a break at the coffee-hatch.

After several thousand years, it was Wednesday. I chose a quiet

76

bar near the Tyne Theatre – a dim place with scarred tables, dark mirrors and, I remembered too late, a floor turned to velcro by spillage and ash. Sylvie accepted a half of Guinness but took only a single sip.

'A bar of dead actors,' she said, looking at the smeary photographs and ghoulish caricatures around the walls. 'And all of those who knew their names are dead as well.'

'Wrong place. I'm sorry –'

'No, it is perfect. There are such bars in Paris. People seek immortality by any means. Some seek it and yet are dead already. There is something you want to ask me, I think.'

'Well, in fact -'

'But how can you drink this – what is it –'

'Guinness. It's good for you.'

'If you say so. Someone I think is lying. Please, I shall have a glass of wine instead.'

Wincing at what she might make of what passed for wine in here, I went up to the bar. The ancient barman smirked.

'Port for the lady is it?'

'Wine. Have you got wine?'

The barman stooped to feel about behind the counter.

'Wine maketh the heart glad,' someone said. My rival stood beside me, tall and at ease, lighting a cigarette. I looked at Sylvie. She smiled in such a way as to suggest that this had been the arrangement all along.

The rival held out a large, calloused hand, white beneath the tobacco stains.

'Christian Dax. And you are Mr Stephen Ash, a famous poet.'

'Not exactly –'

'Give us the bottle and two glasses,' he said to the barman.

'Never any call,' the barman said.

'You surprise me, Monsieur.'

Dax took charge, sitting on the bench beside Sylvie,

pouring her a glass, not offering me one. She softened and brightened in his presence. His head was perfectly shaved, his face pale, his age not young but hard to determine, his teeth large and brown, his eyes unguessable behind the mirrors of the sunglasses.

'So when is your book of poems to be published?' he asked.

'Early days,' I said. 'Who knows – maybe never.' Sylvie wagged her finger at me.

'Too modest,' she said.

'You have read this book?' Dax asked her.

'Some. A little.' This was news to me but on reflection not surprising. It was also a little arousing.

'And does this book matter?'

Sylvie looked down,

'As Stephen says, it is early days.'

'No,' said Dax, agreeably. 'It is late. It is a late era. We have reached the foot of the page. Like the novel, poetry is dead and we cannot go on simply digging it up. Forgive me, Monsieur but we must be truthful, even, as you would say, in "dear old England".'

'I say nothing of the sort, but I hope my poems will be truthful.'

'Then you must write without hope,' Dax said and laughed. 'It is the only way.' I noticed that he was stroking Sylvie's leg, his rough hand snagging in the pale material of her tights. She saw me looking, smiled, bit her lip and moved a little apart from him. He looked at me in amiable challenge, as far as I could tell.

'The future,' he went on, 'is elsewhere than the banal fantasies of the bourgeoisie. We must live fiction and write... whatever remains to be said after the end.'

'So you are a critic?' I asked. He considered.

'Am I a critic? I do not think there is a name for what I am. The taxonomy is incomplete. The work, the practice, the act, has preceded its description.' The brown teeth grinned. 'A theorist, perhaps.'

'What of?'

'De quoi? Of the text, Monsieur. Of the text.'

'Christian is a professor,' Sylvie said, her new demureness to the fore. 'He was my teacher.'

I'll bet he was, I thought.

'And what did he teach you?'

'Oh, I can't remember. It was a long time ago.' They laughed. I joined in, to make up the numbers.

'I taught her about power,' said Dax. 'Who exercises it and who submits before it, and where it lives in language. Language, the world, sex' – Dax's hand was on Sylvie's leg again – 'all these are metonyms of power. The question is who will exert it.'

'Sounds very French,' I said. 'With Nietzsche thrown in.'

'Of course,' he said. Clearly this was too obvious to mention. 'The future, Stephen, will all be Theory,' Dax resumed with sudden urgency. 'Literature as hitherto understood is dead. The author is dead. Humanism itself is dead. We are entering a period of timeless, pitiless modernity. There is nothing outside the text.' I realised that in his affectless way he was elated.

'You are an advocate of disenchantment.'

'Am I?' With an enquiring smile he looked at Sylvie, who was by now watching me anxiously.

'It's all cobblers.'

'Forgive me, but that is hardly an argument. Or perhaps in England it is.'

'Anyway, this 'text' you mention. What is this 'text'?'

'What is it?' he repeated, tolerantly. 'Look around you.'

'This is a pub.'

'And it is terrible, is it not? As the world is terrible.' He smiled again as though his point were proved. 'Recognise that and freedom is possible. If that is what you seek.' He looked at Sylvie, then back at me. 'It is not for everyone.'

With as much grace as I could muster, I excused myself and went to the Gents. I stared into the urinal: Armitage Shanks. There is nothing outside the text. I could think of nothing to do, except to punch Dax repeatedly in the head, which would hardly help matters with Sylvie.

Dax appeared beside me, unzipping his fly. You'll be hung like a fucking horse as well, won't you, Professor Dax? I thought. Balls like a stallion. Oh, yes. It gets better and better.

'There is no need to be afraid of me,' said Dax, inclining his head companionably. He pissed in a powerful continuous stream.

'Afraid of you? I'm not afraid of you, pal. I'm just not sure why you're here.'

'I am not your enemy.'

'No? Well, maybe I'm yours.'

Dax laughed.

'What do you say in your country? "Now wash your hands." That way you will not catch anything.'

We moved in step to the sinks.

'Why are you here?'

'I watch over Sylvie.'

'Bit old for her, aren't you?'

'And you are young.'

'You're just in the way, Dax,' I said. 'You're in the way of Sylvie and me.'

'You think so?' He smiled and soaped his hands carefully. 'You forget, Stephen: I *know* Sylvie. You see her beauty, her charm and freshness. But she is a complicated and vulnerable spirit. And demanding, believe me. But you have suffered a *coup de foudre*. A lightning strike. Except there are no accidents. And now you must love and suffer. You think you've got the – the *balls* for it?'

'Never you mind about that. And there's something else.'

'Please.'

'All this Theory shit. It just means that you can't write, doesn't it? You can't write. You used to, yeah?'

'Long ago. I was like you, a little.'

'I doubt it. And now you can't, so you sneer at other people's work.'

'Is that it?'

If I could not be clever, then I would be dogged.

'All this Theory – it's just smoke and mirrors, isn't it? You're just a parasite.'

'You may be right, Stephen.' Dax produced a small silver dispenser and a tiny mirror, then poured a line of white powder on to the glass. 'Can I show you something?'

'What is that?'

'This? This is white snuff. Very rare.'

'It's coke, isn't it?' Coke itself was a rare thing in those days.

'Coke?' Dax smiled. 'This is better. Try some?'

'After you.' He shrugged, took a banknote from his wallet, rolled it up and snorted the powder in one go. He pursed his lips and breathed out slowly, apparently satisfied. The remnants he rubbed around his gums.

'Try some now? This is a friendly gesture, Stephen. Do not simply reject it. You must change your way of seeing. You must derange your senses, systematically - remember? Then you will see what is there and what is not.'

It is a stupid business at times, being a man. Dax laid out the powder. I used my own fiver and snorted. After a few seconds the back of my head dissolved. I floated free and hung beside myself. I revolved slowly on the ammoniac air of the Gents. In the pattern of green curling waves on the tiling above the sinks I heard the ocean crash and call. Like Ariel I spun the globe by circling it. Silver electricity ran, as if glad to be home, from the tips of my ears to my toes and my penis. I felt as if I was going to turn into half a dozen of me. The world would have to reckon with Stephen Ash.

Then, just as suddenly, the hit wore off. Checkerboards

flashed across my vision. I staggered. This was death, blackness, the pit. Dax held me up with an arm around my shoulders. He laughed.

'Different, eh? White snuff.'

I nodded. My tongue was too big for my mouth.

'Now look in the mirror, Stephen.'

Dax pulled my head upright.

'Look.' I did so. There I was, white as a ghost, but of Dax there was no sign.

'Smoke and mirrors, Stephen. Take care now,' he said, and let me fall.

I had imagined that by the time I collected myself and found my way back into the bar Dax would have folded Sylvie away in his Franco-mobile and vanished into the night. But she was still there, watched by the enraptured barman.

'Christian apologises. He had to leave – he felt a migraine coming on. He suffers badly from them.'

'I'm not surprised.'

'Are you being unkind?'

'I wasn't expecting him in the first place,' I said.

'He is very protective. Like a brother to me.'

'Most brothers don't feel their sisters up. It isn't natural.'

'Really? What is natural?'

'You know what I mean, Sylvie.'

'No, I do not think so.'

'This is stupid. Who is Dax, anyway?'

'My teacher. My… good angel. Believe me.'

'He's a creep.'

'You do not know him as I do.'

'So it would appear.'

'I have not slept with him, Stephen.' I looked at her in shock. She shrugged. 'That is what you wanted to know.'

But she slept with me, under the skylight by the railway,

beginning that night. And Dax became invisible, for a time, and what I wanted most urgently to say to Sylvie about Dax moved from insistence through embarrassment and then began by degrees to look like a drunken figment, a typical trick pulled by a French 'theorist'. Smoke and mirrors.

Love produces innocence and egomania in equal amounts, as Stendhal might have said. The summer world arranged itself about us.

Lovemaking, walking, eating, art galleries, films, the garden flat Sylvie had taken, five minutes from the town. Secret smiles among the stacks of the library, which were not secret at all, but part of a pastoral comedy in which the other staff delightedly conspired, like the princess's ladies in waiting, believing like us in our grove of books and bedsheets, where time had gone on holiday. I can say honestly that I remember happiness, its taste, its encompassing all-generous light.

A letter spelled the end of Paradise. One morning when I came into the kitchen from the little orchard Sylvie had to herself, I found her in tears with a letter in her hand.

'What's wrong?'

She looked at me sadly, as though suddenly aged.

'It is nothing.'

'Clearly it isn't. Is this from Dax? May I see?'

'It is private.'

I swallowed.

'As you wish.'

'Do not be hurt, Stephen.'

'That's difficult, Sylvie.'

'Trust me, though.' She looked at me in appeal. No contest.

I nodded.

'He wants me to return to France with him.'

'Is he in England? In town?'

'He travels always.'

'But Sylvie, he has no claim on you.'

'It is not so simple.'

'You said –'

'And it is true. There is nothing like that between us.'

'Well, then.'

'He needs me.'

'I need you.'

'Yes. And I need you. But in his work, in his essays, I have been – that word – I have been his muse.'

I failed to hide my smirk. Her face fell and she turned away.

'And you were taken in by this, Sylvie? This muse bollocks? He wants to possess you. I said before, it's not natural.'

'You think you know what is natural.'

'It's sick.'

'So everyone is sick.'

'Refuse. Say you want to stay here.'

'He will not accept it.'

'Then I'll explain it to him.'

'That would not be wise. He would be angry.'

'So would I.'

She kissed me.

'I will tell him. I will do as you wish.'

'When?'

'Soon. I want to make love now, Stephen.'

Did the air darken in the days that followed? Did the heat go out of the sun that August? We were waiting. However passionate our lovemaking, it became a fraud, because another, quietly implacable gaze fell on us in that white room and turned it grey and unseasonably cold. I would find Sylvie sitting at her dressing-table, mascara brush in hand, lost, staring through her own face in the mirror as if seeing beyond her own death. A silence fell on the flat. I stopped liking the evening garden.

A second letter came. Again Sylvie would not let me

read it, but I could feel its insistence in the room.

'You've got to tell him.'

'Yes.'

'Or I will.'

'I will tell him soon.'

'Or should I leave, Sylvie? Is that what you want?'

'No, please. But Christian is in pain.'

'Good. He's a parasite. Let him suffer.'

'You don't understand.'

'That's right, Sylvie. I don't. This is hopeless.'

I slammed out of the flat and found myself walking the city for hours. I sat in a pub and thought about nothing.

It was dark when, with my anger exhausted, I went back. I knew immediately that Sylvie was not there, but none of her things were missing. Then I looked on the dressing table and found her compact open with a line of powder laid out on the mirror, in the shape of an *S*. Alongside lay a note in a jagged hand, not hers: *There is nothing outside the text. Courage!* I felt in my pockets for a banknote. In for a penny.

It was gone midnight when I reached the library, the city's revellers for once elsewhere. Mica glittered in the paving stones. Even in the dark the architecture swarmed with details. To look too long would be intolerable, as though the night had turned to one immense and inescapable interior by Piranesi. The tall door was an inch ajar but the stairwell was dark. I had seen Quinn the caretaker unblocking a drain on the pavement with an iron rod he kept in a cubbyhole under the stairs. This too was open. Thus armed, I went up the dark staircase and through the doors by the entrance desk, stopping there to listen but hearing nothing. There was a faint light down at the angle of the gallery. It was very cold. I took the stairs that come out on the upper walkway near the committee room, among tall shelves of dead novels, then moved along until I reached the bridge where the two main rooms are joined.

There was grey, flamy light, but it seemed to have no source. I looked up at the dome and saw stars there but did not recognise the constellation. From below came a soft, keening cry that mixed fear and desire in a way that both appalled and shamefully excited me. Sylvie lay on the marble top of the central radiator as if on an altar, covered in a sheet, her shoulders bare. She seemed uneasily asleep, her face restless, the soft cry repeated. My breath came in a freezing cloud, and the whole immense chamber seemed charged with a terrible and interminable emptiness. I was about to start down the spiral staircase to floor level when a movement distracted me. From behind the clock over the far end of the gallery, Dax seemed to manifest himself as if from nothing. He sprang onto the balustrade and balanced there, barefoot and shirtless, looking down at Sylvie. The glasses were gone. The eyes I will not describe. I hefted the makeshift javelin but knew the distance was too great.

Now Dax looked up through the dome, as if at his private stars, and raised his arms, at which two great black wings unfurled from his shoulders, shuddering with flame, shedding burning feathers to rain on the library floor. He paused like a diver and then, spreading his arms to the side, stepped off the railing and rose with one broad swimming stroke towards the dome. He hung there, ecstatic, revolving in the grey, pitiless light for a moment, before beginning a slow, perfect dive towards Sylvie, fifty feet below. He bared his teeth. He meant, I could see, to drain and consume her.

I must get between them. I stumbled down the last few steps, faintly aware of other figures moving among the stacks. When I reached the altar Dax paused in the air and stood upright, inclining his head.

'Stephen,' he said. 'My faith was justified.'

'Your faith.'

'That you would do your part and be the rescuer. That

is the story.'

'Virtue rewarded.'

'But virtue must suffer misfortune.'

'Why?'

'That is the story also. Move aside and you can watch.' Dax stretched his neck and shook himself. Flakes of fire bounced and slid along the parquet floor. The fires were cold. Dax was their source. I wanted to sleep, to lie down in the freezing flame and sleep for a thousand years.

'Well?' said Dax.

'You can't have Sylvie. You're not the one she wants.'

'Too simple. I can have anything I want. Look around you.'

'I don't care. It's true. That's all that matters.'

'True?' He smiled, unblinking. 'So. And what will you do?'

I hurled the rod. It struck him at the heart and went in deeply. There were gasps around me. For a moment Dax seemed about to collapse on himself, then he steadied and straightened again, reached up with his right hand and pulled the weapon out. He held it at arm's length, and I watched it turn to icy ash and fall away. He had no wound.

'I created Sylvie,' said Dax.

'Your vanity has made you mad.'

'So what?'

'She is a person, not a possession.'

'Are you sure? Is not possession what you desire too?'

'I am capable of love.'

'Love. I have read about that. And so, I understand, you would die for Sylvie. Is that correct? On account of love.'

'If I must. But not today.'

'Bravo. But love belongs in books.' The black wing struck me like a wave of ice.

'I believe you,' said Sylvie.

She stood now, enfolded in Dax's wings. I lay on the

87

floor where I had fallen. Around me I saw Quinn and Miss Greenwell and the other library staff, regarding me with grave attention. They looked like witnesses to an ordeal they must regretfully approve.

'I said: I believe you,' Sylvie repeated, nestling among the feathers.

The drug was wearing off. Objects on the edges of my vision seemed decayed and ordinary, though Quinn, I noticed, was brandishing a cleaver.

'Then tell Dax,' I said. 'Tell Dax and come with me.'

'Dax knows. He laid down the challenge. You accepted and you proved yourself.'

'Worthy of you.'

'Let us say *serious*. Prepared to take a risk.'

'Who are you?'

'I am here. I am Sylvie, your Sylvie.'

She extended a hand. In her palm lay the silver box. She smiled sadly and as she did so my body was charged afresh with oceanic cold. This was Sylvie and it was not. She was the charming ingénue with the touch of mischief, and she was this remoter, melancholy, regal figure, 'as light as love, as ruthless as the Czar' – to whom Dax was merely a devoted courtier, offering his cloak of wings, as though on the steps of a temple.

'Come with me, Stephen. Take the powder.'

'I think I've had enough.'

'No. You have seen only a little. Take it and come with me. There is no time.'

'What is it, Sylvie? Hemlock?'

'Or moly, or St John the Conqueror root, or mandrake. Whatever you like.'

'A dull opiate.'

'Not so dull.'

'Why must I take the powder? May I not come as I am?'

'The third time it is permanent. You will be with us

always.'

'A ménage a trois in Hell?'

'Hell is a name only.'

'And you – what is your name?'

She gave no reply, but I knew – who Sylvie was, what Sylvie was:

Astraea, Cybele, Hecate, Ishtar, Aphrodite, Moneta, Circe, Leukothea, white goddess, inspirer-destroyer of poets. I was no poet, I knew then.

'It will be paradise,' she said. Her eyes were bright with tears. 'Take the powder, Stephen.'

The visual field was decaying now. The globe of light where Dax and Sylvie were standing shrank and intensified.

'Take it,' she said, 'and be with me forever.' She stepped out of Dax's embrace, so close I could have touched her.

'I can't, Sylvie,' I said, not knowing why.

Pity and rage, tenderness and loss passed over her face. She nodded. Dax enfolded her again and raised his head. The freezing light intensified again about the pair and within them. Now they rose towards the starry dome, and Sylvie looked back once towards me. The light exploded with a crash of ice

iii

At this point the manuscript breaks off. Dating the piece has proved difficult. As to what factual elements it may contain among its strenuous fantasies, there was indeed a Sylvie Scarron who worked as a temporary assistant in the library in the summer of 1970, but at this distance in time it has proved impossible to trace her later whereabouts. A member of staff from that time, now living in retirement, recalls that 'she was a pretty girl, a real breath of fresh air, and Stephen Ash did seem keen on her,' but could not say whether any relationship developed. She also remembered that Stephen Ash was excluded from the library after a drunken argument with the caretaker sometime in the autumn of that year. Of Christian Dax no trace has been found.

Features of the Text

1

It was twenty years ago. In the Literature Departments of the English-speaking world, Literary Theory was approaching its imperious and all-consuming climax. Value was dead and meaning [was] unwell. Radical scepticism, deconstruction and intertextuality seemed like the new Tables of the Law – or they would have done if that Mosaic comparison had not exemplified everything Theory sought to abolish – such as stability, authority and even the idea of truthfulness itself. All this sounds rather solemn, but for some it was a very sexy time: the book, or rather, 'the text', offered a kind of burlesque, a superior striptease, an undressing to the final veil, and perhaps beyond.

Two bright young people sat in a pub at the end of the working day, arguing. Their conversation was a courtship, of a kind. In the best contemporary manner, they had already had the sex. Now came the analysis, the verbal love-play, the thing whose absence from a book Alice could not understand: that is, conversation.

'Yes, yes, *in theory*,' Nicolette Kennaway said, 'there is nothing outside the text.'

'In theory,' replied Alaric Cope, 'there is no context in which to use the phrase "in theory".'

'Yes, but you know what I mean.'

'Do I?'

'You know you do.' Nicolette drank some wine. It was the empty time in the Bodega, after six and before the evening crowd. The terrible bony hobbled music of the time ground away quietly. The barmaids were looking at baby pictures. Down at the far end, under the other dome, relieved of a lifetime of intellectual obligations, the retired Professor of Poetry with the exploding grey hair was subjecting a crumpled copy of *The Sporting Life* to an exhaustive reading. No one should approach him. When he had finished the paper and his fourth pint of Workie Ticket he would leave, pausing with a surprised smile to say he wished he'd seen the two postdoctoral fellows before. They must get together sometime soon. It was a routine. It was human nature, but neither of the young people believed there was any such thing. They didn't find the Professor very convincing, either. To have thought otherwise would have laid them open to the suspicion of essentialism. The old Professor would have to make do with being a feature of the text. He seemed happy enough in his condition.

Alaric slipped his hand under Nicolette's skirt, stroking her thigh at the top of her blue stocking.

'Alaric, of course you know what I mean,' said Nicolette, smiling, but turning away on the bench as though displeased, displacing his hand. 'Anyway, it's your round.'

As Alaric stood at the bar, he looked back at Nicolette. The blonde bell of her hair masked her face as she leaned forward, flicking through the afternoon's seminar paper. Her skirt, just above the knee, was bright red, like a defiant, self-assured laugh. She was a very clever girl, Alaric thought, but mostly he wanted to go to bed with her again, and he wasn't sure if it was going to happen. In his personal affairs he abhorred uncertainty, though in matters of work it was the element where he happily swam, an extension of pleasure towards the infinite. Now he longed to swim between Nicolette's long brown legs. He realised the barmaid was staring at him. He apologised and paid.

'Yes,' he said, sitting down again. 'I know what you mean when you say "in theory". But imagine a sort of literary-critical Year Zero, when all the exits have been sealed, and we address the –'

'We address the facts, you were about to say.' Nicolette gave her wonderful scarlet-lipped bedroomy smile. 'But in your Year Zero, all the distracting and misleading assumptions have been purged away, when the "world" –' (here she drew quotation marks in the air) '– and the text are indivisible and have always been so, when all this –' (she gestured to take in the room and what lay beyond it) '– is not even the memory of an illusion, and has "in fact" never existed, by what name will you call these "facts" then?'

'I love it when you talk dirty,' he said. She held his gaze, still smiling, requiring a proper answer. 'Obviously,' he went on, 'the text – and by "the text" I mean you and me - the text will produce the vocabulary to meet the need.'

'I wonder,' said Nicolette, looking into her wine glass. 'I wonder if the text will be adequate, whether it will be able to reproduce its initial effect' – she took his hand and placed it back on her leg, guiding his fingers under the edge of the stocking – 'or indeed whether we should ask it, or even wish it, to do so.'

'I wonder,' said Alaric.

2

Every chance, as it turned out. But it was a bad business in the end. Alaric's *jouissance* was short-lived. Firstly it turned out that Nicolette was also sleeping with Ramon, a wordless computational linguist from the Dead Zone down on the first floor of the Department.

'Does it bother you?' she asked.

'We are free subjects. Or we aspire to be,' Alaric said.

'Debatable, I'd say, but does it bother you?'

Alaric shrugged and went to the bar.

Secondly, Nicolette was also *also* sleeping with Michelle, a PhD student. Alaric reckoned he could have handled this if he'd been allowed to watch. It would have been, well, it would have been Foucauldian, sort of, but he dared not even enquire about the matter.

'People will think you're a bike,' he said.

'As long as they can work the gears,' replied Nicolette. 'Anyway, they *already* think you're a prick. It's your round again, by the way.' She leaned forward and took his hand and kissed him lingeringly just beneath the ear.

Her self-assurance seemed to Alaric quite impenetrable. There were no side entrances. It seemed that Nicolette the theorist was never off-duty. Not only did she determine who would receive her sexual favours: increasingly it seemed to him that she had the power to confirm or deny the identity of others; for example him, Alaric. Alone on empty evenings in his room near Spital Tongues he could not quite believe in his ontological integrity. Had he grown weak, in secret from himself? He had come to feel as though Nicolette were in some sense *his author*. In her periods of absence, or when she capriciously withdrew her approval (she never explained, never apologised) he could feel himself thinning and fading, losing texture and outline. One day soon, he feared, he would look in the mirror and instead of his face see only the bookcase that stood against the opposite wall, baring its brown teeth at him. He told himself he'd been overworking.

Nicolette would deny this authorial role, of course, since as they both well knew, the author was dead. He could never raise the matter with her: she would simply find it amusing. To be the object of her laughter would be intolerable. Her power seemed to reside in her very lack of interest in oppressing or controlling him. Like a character in a nineteenth century novel, he might seem to an imagined reader to be at liberty to leave at any time and go his own way - except that, equally clearly, he wasn't. He was being written; more, he feared he would eventually be written out.

As spring slipped towards summer he found himself walking home through the green streets at dawn once or twice a week, expelled from Nicolette's bed with the sweetest smile because she liked to make an early start on her work. The frequency and regularity of her summons gave him no assurance that it would continue. His work stalled. Then – it was Midsummer's Eve – he found himself impotent.

'You'd better go,' said Nicolette.

'What?'

'I don't want you to be embarrassed.'

'What?'

'It's for the best.'

'I'll tell you what this is,' he said, gesturing at his groin as he struggled into his jeans. 'You're reifying me.'

Nicolette shook her head in disbelief. 'Believe me, sweet, if I was *reifying* you, if I was *objectifying* you, we wouldn't be having this trouble.'

'You know what I mean.'

'If you say so. Let yourself out. I'll ring you.'

She didn't, of course. Neither did she write or come round. Alaric was left to imagine Nicolette's bumper sessions with Ramon, Michelle, or both, plus unnamed others. His room was like a giant box of used tissues. He thought he might go mad, supposing he didn't disappear first. Several times a day he sneaked up on the mirror to check he was still in there. He felt like a work of art too often reproduced, its aura worn away. Behind him the books on the shelf massed at his fraying border.

The day he destroyed Nicolette he had come into the Department, allegedly to collect his post but actually in the hope of seeing her and pleading his cause. In recent weeks she had vanished from this world, this hell, of her own creation – a *dea* wholly *abscondita*, leaving not even the mocking intoxication of her laughter on the dry air of the departmental corridors.

Today he noticed that the door of her office was open. He peeped inside. There was no one in the neat, bright room. Her bag and her jacket were missing. She must be at lunch or in the library. He inhaled her scent, and stood for a moment in the perfection of despair, looking down into the courtyard. To be standing here in her empty room was, Alaric thought with a sob, the confirmation that he was no longer a participant in the text. He had indeed been written out. He was over.

As he made to turn away, he saw Nicolette come into view, leaving by the main doors of the department arm in arm with two figures he instantly recognised as Ramon and Michelle. Nicolette's car was parked by the archway. The trio climbed in, with Ramon in the back, and Nicolette drove away. She would not be back in a minute or an hour or that afternoon, Alaric saw. In her besotted state she had simply forgotten to lock her office door. On her desk was an A4 envelope addressed to go out. She had forgotten that as well.

3

In their tentative manner, the members of the department reached the same conclusion as the Coroner, that Nicolette Kennaway had taken her own life while the balance of her mind was disturbed. The coroner left it at that, but in the further informal post-mortems conducted in various Jesmond kitchens her former colleagues did honour to the requirements of Literary Theory by which Nicolette had lived. They made the evidence stand on its head. Nicolette's characteristic and unfailing cheerfulness thus became a sign of an inner abyss from which despair came slithering to claim her. Her efficiency both as a teacher and an administrator was a sign of psychic disorder. Her well-received first book on Lacan and her frequent essays and papers betrayed frustration and self-loathing. Ergo. Was her death a tragedy? Perhaps. Did it offer a lesson? Surely. But what about?

Alaric Cope listened to several of these discussions but kept his counsel. He had troubles enough of his own. He had not really thought through his intervention in the story of himself and Nicolette. He had acted opportunistically from a kind of desperate spite simply to ensure his own continued

96

presence. He had failed to plan, and his improvisation sprang narrative traps of a kind that could not be reversed. She was dead, and he, well, he appeared to be damned.

In the envelope which Nicolette had left on her desk that fateful lunchtime was the proof of an essay on George Eliot waiting to be returned to a leading journal of Victorian cultural materialism. Alaric read the piece and saw his revenge. He made a handful of tiny alterations to a couple of paragraphs in the text, meticulously forging Nicolette's fastidious hand. Then he replaced the essay in the envelope, which he sealed and left in the posting tray in the secretaries' office.

It was almost a year before the essay appeared in the august journal, and a further six months before a brief but damning letter from another scholar, based elsewhere but not wholly unknown to Alaric, followed the essay into print. There was, he had to admit, a dark splendour in managing to suggest that Nicolette had stolen someone's intellectual property in a sphere where the very idea of originality was frequently derided.

Plagiarism is extremely hard to prove, but the suggestion of it lingers and the stain is hard to eradicate. In due course, and perhaps for other reasons entirely, Nicolette was turned down for a permanent post in the department. If Alaric regretted this, he none the less took some satisfaction in his own successful appointment. Then Nicolette went off the Tyne Bridge, striking The Boat a glancing blow as she fell, and he had not meant that at all.

The dreams were bad enough. Night after night he would be staring at a page of dense print which would then gradually re-form itself to reveal Nicolette's smiling post-coital face, made up of thousands of repetitions of her name. Not content with this, the dream determined that this face of words should assume three dimensions, like a death mask made out of 12-point Times New Roman. And the sweet, terrible mask of Nicolette would open its mouth to speak.

And he would wake up, knowing that whenever he next slept he would undergo this dream again, confined to this one inescapable text, the dead but mobile face of his lover.

Dreams are one thing. The waking world is another. Alaric managed to live there successfully with his guilt. If he drank a little more and grew a little haggard nobody mentioned it. He lived alone and his colleagues at work had the semi-autistic preoccupations of academics everywhere. There were texts to be edited, interrogated, dismantled and subjected to further novel torments thrown up by the great invasive tide of Theory. He stuck it out. What else could he do? It was a mild relief to accept the dinner invitations that in the days when he was sleeping with Nicolette he would have turned down without thinking.

He could even stand the post mortems. People would turn to him in mid-discussion, abashed by his silence and yet curious, and say, 'But Alaric, you knew her well. Were there no signs?'

'Alas, no,' he would reply, lowering his gaze in sorrowful bafflement. Nicolette's sorrows had obviously lain beyond the reach even of her friends. A tragedy. A lesson of some kind.

And so it went on as he made his way around the kitchens of the departmental womenfolk, the subject dying off a little over time, as everything does. He relaxed, in that waking world.

Then after an interval the matter came up one more time, in one more kitchen, half-heartedly, as though the company were journalists needing the story to grow more legs. It was fizzling out, until someone said, 'There's no art to find the mind's construction in the face.' There were noises of agreement around the table. Alaric felt very hot, then very cold, and became afraid he would faint. Thankfully no one noticed. He excused himself and went to the bathroom.

He locked the door and ran water into the sink, then immersed his face for half a minute. He reached for a towel and dried his face, before looking in the mirror. There she was, her beautiful face drawn in print and dead white, joyful, three-dimensional, on the brink of speech, as to a lover in the afterglow. His own face was nowhere to be seen. She had won again. She had replaced him.

He turned away and breathed deeply. Hallucination. Stress. Drink. Exhaustion. Guilt. A symptom, not a fact. He unlocked the door and went downstairs, counting slowly, regulating his breathing. In a moment he would be back in company and this episode would pass. It was some kind of flashback. He avoided the mirror in the hallway, paused, then opened the kitchen door. As he did so, he saw immediately that his loss of face (he laughed, high-pitched, at this idea) was the least of his worries, when the faces of the others turned smiling towards him, death-pale, swarming with print, all of them Nicolette.

Close to You

You were giving a public lecture one October evening. It was part of a series tracing the development of the horror genre from the eighteenth century onwards. You had reached Joseph Sheridan Le Fanu, author of the turgid novel *Uncle Silas* and the incomparable short story 'Carmilla'. Although it was a miserable night, there was quite a sizeable crowd to listen to you, and to watch you, as you stood before the long table beneath the clock. They were your usual audience, enthusiasts of the supernatural, fans of your authority and of your crisp elegance. You wore that black suit and the wine-coloured shirt, with a dark rose in your buttonhole.

As you spoke, you barely consulted your notes. It was your area. You knew a great deal about many subjects, but these stories - Beckford, Lewis, Mrs Radcliffe, Mary Shelley, Maturin and Le Fanu - were the place in which you really lived. Some might call it rather an arid district. Your audience would have disagreed. They were right. They adored you, Dr Sheridan (no relation) – Lisa – just as they adored the old library, with its domes and alcoves and galleries and dim staircases. For them it was a treat to sit and listen to you in these surroundings, to be as though part of the text of the greater book whose margins you were exploring on their behalf. Who would fail to admire the audience's uncluttered pleasure?

I remember your words as though by heart. I hear the assured, husky music of your voice and delivery. You said:

'It has been plausibly suggested that the remote Austrian

setting of his story *Carmilla* is actually used by the Protestant Sheridan Le Fanu, knowingly or not, as a means of displacing and encoding the anxieties of the Ascendancy class in nineteenth century Ireland. The heroine's home, her father's castle, stands at the edge of an immense brooding forest. The forest is a steady subliminal presence in the story. It creates fear even before the narrative is properly under way. It is the outside that wants to come in. And it is out of this forest that the coach comes, bearing its deadly passenger. In a sense, *Carmilla* is as much concerned with anticipation as with action. This is of course true of all stories, but the presence of the forest, even when not specifically mentioned, acts as a kind of undertow, drawing both the heroine and the reader ever closer to the source of her anxieties. That source is, of course, the mysterious companion who has been inexorably approaching since – we may say – the day she was born.'

If only you knew.

I happened along that evening a year or two back. For some considerable time I had been travelling in Europe. I came discreetly ashore at evening and entered the city. As I made my way up from the quayside, smoky yellow light fell from the library's doorway and windows on to the rainy pavement. The venerable Palladian frontage stirred my interest. So in I went, up the stairs and in past the issue desk, up the side stairs to the shelved gallery, and there you were. You had paused on the main floor below, talking to the librarian, your head thrown back in amusement at some joke, your cloud of black ringlets settling again as your mood changed and you spoke with sudden stern emphasis and a flash of your green eyes. Here the librarian herself burst out laughing and the pair of you walked away and round the corner where your public was urgently waiting.

That night and for the rest of the series I watched from the top of the spiral staircase as you worked your magic. Your lectures made the unreadable (not to mention the factually erroneous) take on a three-dimensional life. The effect was to send your listeners scurrying to the stacks for books hitherto so long unconsulted that their pages had adhered to one another in the blue-clouded atmosphere of a library where – what enlightenment! – smoking was still permitted. I watched all this and smoked a Special Turkish myself as you moved regally among your people. For the first time in longer than I cared to remember, I found myself interested. The Europe that could contain you could not be dismissed as the ash and waste I believed it had become. I breathed your name out in a smoke-ring, up into the dome. *Lisa*: say it softly – charm, summons, enchantment, whisper of threat. Your life changed on that evening, though of course you were not privy to the fact.

After all this Gothic literature, I ought not to have been surprised to discover that you lived in a castle. It was thirty miles north of the city, out in the hills, at the end of an unnumbered road, within shouting distance of the border. The building was a fifteenth century stone Pele tower with additions, overlooking a small lake ringed with willows. You occupied the tower, naturally. Absentee managerial types intermittently camped out in the remainder, but mostly you had the place to yourself, which was clearly how you preferred it. You liked the lake and its willow-fringe for walks, dawdling by the rush-beds as you declined to accept the importunings of various former and would-be lovers on your mobile phone. You sat at your study window reading and looking out to the northwest across the Debatable Lands, while the restless weather endlessly revised itself from gale to sleet to shafts of otherworldly sunlight. You wrote, without tiring, week after week, your book on the Gothic. The title was *The Gothic Reviv'd* (that made me smile). Beyond your window, on the nearest ridge, the forest of pines stood like an army awaiting a command, untired by centuries of patience. You kept up your work, marking student papers, preparing your lectures. You drove into the University to perform your duties with that crisp, lightly-worn but insatiable efficiency which won such wide admiration – and more than admiration - from smitten students of both sexes. Not that you gave any sign of noticing.

The School of English was developing a name as a centre for the study of the Gothic on the strength of your work: eager postgraduates came in growing numbers. A Chair must soon (and deservedly) be yours, or surely you would be gone into the great world. America was taking an interest. I did not like the sound of that. Were you tempted? Whereas most people have no self at all to speak of really, it was pleasingly difficult to know your mind. At any event you did not neglect your more general and adoring public at the library. You commanded, as it were, both the tower and the plain. You were, in short, and unlike the heroines of so many of the books in your field, strikingly self-possessed. And that, Lisa, that was the hook.

There was one who persisted, one who actually penetrated the tower itself. He was a doctor, a psychiatrist. His name was Richard. He was good-looking, I suppose, in a wheat-pale, absent-mindedly athletic way. In my view he was never a candidate for the long haul. He lacked fire. Good was all he was. But for once you were too polite to make your dissatisfaction known, and he was on the scene for some months, turning up on Friday afternoons in his Land Rover with a bottle of wine or a bunch of wrong-coloured roses. I wonder what it was about Richard. He tried too hard. He was a good listener, I grant you, but only because he had nothing to say. Was he an impressive lover? I did not look into that. When he was still there as Christmas approached, I was worried that you might make a serious error of judgement.

Richard had an accident. On a sleety evening on his way home he misjudged a downhill bend – the brakes of his vehicle may have failed – and crashed through a wooden gate before the vehicle sank into a small lake. The lake was not very deep, and Richard might well have escaped to safety: but as he struggled ashore he was beaten to death with a large stone. The authorities whispered to each other that the corpse was barely recognisable. It was true.

You were distraught. I could understand that, up to a point. It is easy to overrate these attachments, to take the wish for the fact, as easy as to allow guilt to resemble love. It took you several months to begin to recover. After that you no longer permitted suitors to approach you at home. The telephone blinked their red-eyed despair. The chatelaine wisely wedded herself to solitude. I could afford to wait. The apt moment would present itself. Then you would learn, once and for all, the true nature of passion, of possession. Your white Irish skin would flush with rose. All in good time.

I said it was difficult to know your mind. Yet I was shocked that you betrayed me, Lisa. I am surprised by my own negligence. It was in the book, the one you were writing, *The Gothic Reviv'd*: that was where you betrayed me. Somehow it took me a long time to actually get around to dipping into it. I suppose I thought of the book as simply a superior prop in the erotic drama we were, in a sense, contriving together. I thought of writing as something for you to do in the meantime. Your book was like the book someone is writing in a film – the work which exists only as the illegible upside-down page at which the heroine, her hair oh-so-casually pinned up, directs her intent gaze. The camera pans across her desk, pausing lovingly over her noble downturned face before stopping to peer out of the window at the shaggy green-black camouflage ranks of the forest, still waiting along the hill-ridge, bristling with alert discretion. The air out there is piny and expectant.

Because when it comes, the action will not be a matter of words and pages and references and revision and the drainpipe-grey bureaucracy of knowledge, but something more urgent and physical. When that day is here we shall do no more reading. This is the contract between watcher and watched. It is the iron law of the story, and of this story in particular.

I ponder that phrase, 'the people of the book'. Philistines view literature as an escape. They are correct, but for the wrong reasons. The book is an escape, but the realm it offers to open would be too rich for the blood of the unthinking. Their minds would simply dissolve on impact. Believe me. More important, if the world contained no books, but only the memories of print, thoughtful people such as yourself would understand more fully the energies that books serve to discharge. They would see that these forces are at least as potent as actual laughter and sex and the apprehension and free contemplation of death. They would weep their loss, for a time. But I put it to you, darling Lisa, that quite soon they would turn to embrace the ecstasy of the animals, or of the gods. Consider the fate of the patron saints of critics such as yourself. This ecstasy is what Nietzsche meant (and at the death, as you know, he literally embraced a horse). This ecstasy is what killed Foucault, it seems, when he immersed himself in the destructive element where blood meets semen.

When I discovered your infidelity, when at last it occurred to me actually to read your book, you had more or less finished it. This was the book which would make your name not only in but beyond the academy. You would 'cross over' into 'the real world', as ignorant people like to call it. My own journey was not dissimilar in some respects.

Imagine my surprise! To put it plainly, you were an unbeliever. I searched the work repeatedly, in vain, for a glimmer of acknowledgement of how things stand between the tale and the reader, but in the end I had no choice but to conclude that as far as you were concerned the story was *a story*. And a story was a means of – for example - encoding and dramatising the spiritual, social, economic and sexual anxieties of a particular period blah de blah. And the tale could be compelling, enthralling, richly mysterious and erotic – you said yes, yes, to all of that – but in the last analysis the tale was only a work of the imagination rather than a symbolic intimation of the forces actually in stormy, lustful, exultant and impatient play on the other side of the page. The story was *only a story*. The sharp-toothed insinuating Carmilla, she who could materialise in a room unbidden, whose swaying, weightless movement was its own dark beguiling music, she who would provoke in her beloved a languor of desire whose musky sweetness brought a near-intolerable pleasure - Carmilla had no more substance than the paper she was written on. She was a play of signs, a figment of ink got up to amuse the recently literate and the newly bored in the discreet purgatory of nineteenth century bourgeois constraint! And I was likewise imaginary, a dream without purchase or consequence. As I say, imagine my surprise. Oh, dear. Lisa, Lisa. This is a terrible pity. How could you?

I have spoken of the forces in attendance behind the page. When I read of the amusement with which you regarded my kind, I myself had to undergo an education of sorts, to rediscover – for there is nothing truly new - that anger, pain and desire may in fact be synonyms. I studied carefully, dwelling at length in that extremity, as though at prayer – if one can be said to pray to oneself. After a time I could almost have wished to be other than myself; almost. But life, as you call it, goes on, or the story does. And here we are.

So. When you address the mirror at night to remove that just-so shade of crimson lipstick, I am looking back at you, Lisa. I am there in the silver of the glass. When you undress to bathe, I am the air itself upon your limbs and the sudden soft breath that makes you pause and turn for a moment as you reach for the towel. When you draw back the bed-covers and slip between the sheets, naked except for those severe half-moon spectacles, I am there to observe from the four-poster's canopy while you settle to reading. Often, darling, you fall asleep without removing your spectacles, the book still open on your breast. I could put both spectacles and book on the bed-side table if I wished; I do indeed wish, but

I resist, for that is more exciting.

I can wait a long time, though you, alas, do not have forever. You write books because you must die. That fact is no more imaginary than I am. One day I shall have to give in. You think I am a metaphor? You think? God is not mocked, my love, and neither am I. Desire and the clock have made an appointment, and when that night comes we shall see what is real and what imagined.

Kiss Me Deadly
on the Museum Island

I would be prepared to bet a large sum that the works of Mickey Spillane are not represented in the library. Mike Hammer? Mr Hardboiled himself. *Of course*, you might say, *his day is gone. History found him insufficiently interesting.* History? You mean librarians. *Or insufficiently hardboiled. You should read some of the stuff they get in nowadays: enough to make your pubes stand on end.* If you say so.

I was about to explain my own involvement in the works of the creator of Mike Hammer. And I discover to my alarm that the episode in question took place fifteen years ago, in 1989. I was a young man, recently appointed in the Department, immersed in my studies, eager for anywhere they might take me. A man of the Left, also, as they say in Europe. A sentimentalist, as we say nowadays; but I have never understood that word completely.

My subject was the brothers Mann, Heinrich and Thomas – the socialist and the nationalist, the satirist and the elegist, the victim and the survivor, the implacably twinned authors of *Man of Straw* and *Doktor Faustus*. What was my subject, really? I think it was probably the idea of my own seriousness against a historical backdrop of vast terror and exhilaration. Anyway. That April I was due to take part – in my other persona, which it may surprise you to hear was that of poet - in a translation seminar. This was held at a conference centre in Glienicke, in West Berlin, near the famous Bridge of

Spies. Inbound for Tegel, the plane seemed to me to descend on the very core of Europe. There it lay in the green spring chill, the sandy lakes and the Grunwald and all those loaded names – Potsdam, Spandau, Wannsee, and the political island of the city itself. Speaking objectively, who could resist? Has anyone ever managed to do so? Who would not be enchanted by the way the Wall itself ran through the middle of the outbuildings of this old hunting lodge? Who would not be beguiled by the bucolic menace of a Vopo patrol boat nosing along through the Death Zone of the lake?

Then I fell in love, there by the lake in the woods where signs – You Are Now Leaving the American Zone - stand knee-deep in the water: and where at dawn you may hear the melodic hysteria of the nightingales.

Steffi was a translator, a freelance brought in through the offices of one of the cultural organisations lending its support to the conference. She had the sallow, slightly sluttish good looks you find among dark-haired German girls, along with a harsh smoker's laugh and an intense professional seriousness about Rilke and Holderlin and Brecht that was just as arousing as the legs she wrapped around me when the nightingales began their blue jazz.

We never missed a seminar all week. I don't remember sleeping; nor do I remember how the affair got under way. I remember her room – books, papers, overflowing ashtrays, scattered underwear, and her critical but encouraging gaze from beneath her fringe as she sat astride me, urging me to redouble my efforts. She would come with a harsh groan, lie back for a minute, then light her umpteenth cigarette.

'I'll end up smoking if I stay with you,' I told her once.

'That's good. I'm looking for converts.'

'Do you have a preferred brand? *Roth Handle?*'

'Na. I smoke anything. The point is to smoke, to be engaged in smoking. You should have a shower.'

110

'Really?'

'You stink.'

'Then I stink of you.'

'It's a labour of love,' she said, then closed her eyes against the smoke.

On the last evening of the conference we absconded from the regimented dining room to a place in the woods – beer and sausage for political tourists in the chilly lanterned arbour where we talked as a prelude to further bouts of sex. Steffi was from the East. Her parents got out just before Ulbricht sealed the border. She had never seen her grandparents or aunts or uncles, all still living in Leipzig. She was a woman of the Left, she said; Maoist, not Stalinist, of course.

'The distinction's academic, isn't it? Really?' I said. She gave me one of her looks. 'I mean, I sympathise, of course, but given the location, the present tendency of history and so on –'

'Fuck you, Richard,' she said equably. 'History? History has nothing to do with you. You're a tourist, remember. Worse, you're English. Finish your dinner.'

I was drunk and could not keep my mouth shut.

'What will we do now that it's over – the conference?'

She shrugged and blew smoke in my face.

'You will go back, I suppose.'

'Not necessarily.'

'You should not overrate this experience. Yes, I am as you say a lovely fuck. But I am not England.'

'I don't want England.'

'You will.'

'I'll be the judge of that.'

She smiled and reached for my hand.

'All the women in my family tell fortunes as well as being Marxists. This line –' she squeezed my palm roughly, like a masseuse – 'is for love. And this –' again, harder – 'is for brains.'

'And what do you conclude?'

'That if your brains were as big as your cock you would be another Hegel.'

'Well, that's something.'

She gathered her things together and stood up.

'Let's go tonight,' she said.

'What? And miss the final plenary?'

'Regrettably, yes.'

'Where shall we go?'

'I'll take you to my place.'

I had not thought of Steffi as having a *place*. I suppose I thought she simply manifested herself in a professional context from time to time and inbetweenwhiles vanished. I began to explain this.

'Well, let's find out,' she said. That was her Trabant in the car park. As we drove through the dark she pointed out of the window and said, 'That's where they did it.'

'What is?'

'Wannsee. The Wannsee Conference.' Somehow ashamed, I stared into the dark and saw nothing. 'That is why Comrade Ulbricht punished everyone. It was for our own good.' She laughed.

Steffi lived in Kreuzberg, near GropiusStadt, in a street of Turkish grocers and cafes, in a tall, ancient-looking block with no lights in the lobby. The lift was antique and very slow. She put her head against my chest and we crawled upwards through the creaking dark, through smells of cooking and sounds of radio music and other people's domesticity.

'This is as far as we go,' she said, leading me across a corridor under a faintly orange skylight. Music came through the door of the apartment. She unlocked the door and called, 'Irmgard, is that you?'

I had not expected Irmgard. Irmgard might be an impediment to the urgent final intimacy I think I was seeking. There was no reply. A door at the end of the hall opened on to a large room. The far wall taken up by a window, beyond which lay a balcony. The glass door to the balcony was open. We went out. Steps led down to a roof area with, unexpectedly, a pool, in which a woman was swimming laps. She saw us, stopped and took off her pink goggles. We approached.

'Richard, this is Irmgard. She is a lesbian.'

'Excellent,' I said, reminding myself of William Whitelaw.

'Richard is a poet.'

'Well –' I began.

'Another one?' said Irmgard, climbing effortlessly from the pool to stand streaming on the tiles. 'I thought you were finished with them.'

'Richard is different,' said Steffi, laughing. She handed Irmgard a towel.

'As you wish, Liebchen,' said Irmgard. 'Would you excuse me, Richard?' She towelled her blonde hair fiercely and went indoors.

'I feel I'm intruding,' I said.

'Don't worry about Irmgard. She feels protective towards me. It is her way.'

'And do you need her to protect you?'

'Let's have a drink.'

We sat on the settee drinking beer. The evening seemed to be running out of steam. I wondered if I should have come. Irmgard reappeared in street clothes. She smiled awkwardly, then looked expectantly at Steffi.

'Well?'

'Not yet. We have only just arrived.'

'You must try,' said Irmgard. 'I must go to work.'

'What do you do?'

'I work in a nightclub,' she said.

When Irmgard had gone I asked, 'What kind of nightclub?'

'Not the sort you imagine.'

'Pardon me.'

'Not like some filthy Kirchner painting. It is a comedy

113

club. A club of satirists and small plays of the Left, even sometimes of poets. Irmgard says she works there. In fact she owns it. This flat is hers. I am her tenant. Are you disappointed?' Steffi smiled and laughed her racking laugh.

'Should I have come here, though? I mean really.'

'Let me show you.'

As it began to grow light there was no sign of Irmgard.

'Have you been across the wall? You must have,' Steffi said.

'No. I was planning to.'

'Today? Then you must go.'

'But what about you?'

She smiled.

'I have work, Richard. I am not so economically autonomous that I can spend my whole life fucking, not even with you.'

'I don't want to waste time I could spend with you.'

'Why? Is this a holiday romance?'

'I hope not.'

'I will be here when you return. After that we shall see.'

'If you're sure.'

'Go to East Berlin, Richard. Walk around. It may not be there forever.'

'That's not what I've heard.'

'You could do me a favour.'

'Of course.'

'I need you to take something through with you.'

'I'm sorry?'

'It's a small thing only.'

'Wouldn't that be dangerous?'

'Hardly. No matter. Forget it.' She smiled and went through into the kitchen. I followed. She filled the coffee pot and stared out of the window.

'I'm sorry,' I said. 'You caught me –'

'Off guard. So I see.' Again the unbearably sweet smile that said: *You're only human. Like the others. Like those other poets here before you.*

'I suppose I am worried in case it's dangerous,' I said. She shrugged, smiled again and busied herself with cups. 'Is it dangerous?'

'What can I tell you, Richard? There is a tiny risk, yes. I should not have asked. We will forget it.'

Oh no we won't. This failure of yours will be our definition, you coward.

'What is it you want me to carry through?'

'It no longer matters.' She handed me a cup and went into the living room.

'Just tell me,' I said, my embarrassment crossing over into anger. Tried and found wanting.

She studied me as she lit a cigarette.

'Sure?'

I nodded.

'It is a book.'

'What kind of book?'

'A small one.'

'I mean, what is it about?'

'I have not read it.'

'For fuck's sake, Steffi.'

'So. Our first argument.'

'Can I see it?' She went to the shelves and came back with a small paperback. 'Let me see.'

It was a 1952 first edition paperback of *Kiss Me Deadly*.

'Is this a joke?'

She shrugged.

'Is it?' I repeated.

'To you perhaps.'

'This is a pulp crime novel. It's hardly – I dunno – Hayek or Friedman, is it?

'*De gustibus*,' said Steffi.

'I'm not sure the censors would agree with you there.

Anyway, have you read it?'

'It is not for me.'

'Of course. Then who is it for?'

'My uncle.'

I saw the uncle sitting in his vest at his tower block kitchen table, longing for the garbage of the Fascist West.

'Fuck. Why this?'

'Ask him.'

'Perhaps I will. I mean, this isn't even really pornography.'

'Have you read it?'

'No.'

'Then how can you tell what it is?'

'I just know.'

'How convenient.' She opened the window and let in a blast of chill air. 'So are you refusing because you are frightened, or on the grounds of taste?'

'I didn't say I was refusing.'

'Are you sure?'

'Why does your uncle want this book?'

'That's not your concern.'

'It is if I have to carry the book across the border.'

'"The border!" Whoooo! "The border!"' She waved her arms in a ghostly way. 'Quick, everyone! Run before the giant crabs devour us!'

'Now you're being silly.'

'What is it? You want me to suck your cock? OK.'

'No – I mean, yes, but not for that reason.'

'You are a confused boy, Richard.'

'Why does your uncle – supposing he is your bloody uncle – want this crappy book?'

She looked at me from under her fringe.

'Because in addition to being a professor of history he likes pulp crime novels. Hank Janson, Peter Cheyney, James Hadley Chase. And Mickey Spillane above all. Don't ask me why. Why did Stalin like Chaplin?'

'That's not the same.'

'So will you take it for me?'

'That's all? No funny business?'

'Who am I, Richard?'

'We've scarcely been introduced, darling.'

'Yes, but what am I? Olga Bendova the beautiful spy, screwing my way to the final triumph of capitalism and/or Actually Existing Socialism? Is that what you think?'

'Of course not.'

'Well, then, Richard, the conclusion seems evident. Either you are a coward, or you take a teeny-tiny little risk. You think they waste time searching tourists?'

We parted at the front door. We would rendezvous at the flat in the evening.

Checkpoint Charlie? Checkpoint Charlie was simply an indoor queue. The hare-eyed young guards looked through me.

Released into the wide, empty streets of Mitte I tried to summon appropriate feelings. The corner of a huge nineteenth century block – warehousing, offices, nothing at all but partitioned shadows? – was pocked with bullet holes. It looked like a grey cheese. Posters on chained gateways showed the Party lists for the forthcoming elections. Greedy for more actuality I wandered a little way north and found a workmen's café where I ate a piece of rubbery torte, watched neutrally by two middle-aged waitresses from the curtained kitchen doorway.

This indulgence meant I had to rush to meet Professor Gisevius. But I was the first one to arrive among the sooty domes of the Museum Island. The air was thick with the smell of coal. Though the day was chilly I was sweating into my shirt. I leaned on the parapet and looked into the grey river's waters. So far there was nothing wrong, was there? I was a tourist, taking in the major landmarks. At any moment

I could go home if I chose. I could throw the damn book in the river.

'Herr Doktor Richard Joyce?'

Professor Gisevius had come up silently, like a barge on the dark water. He tilted his head with a questioning smile, a fit-looking man of sixty-odd with thick white hair and silver-rimmed spectacles. He wore a heavy black coat.

'Professor Gisevius?'

'Good. Let us go. It is cold today, I think.'

'Where shall we go?'

'There is an office. There we can talk and take refreshments.'

'I don't want to be too long.'

'Naturally.' He gestured ahead. A black Wartburg drew up at the kerb and the driver got out. A solid, fair young man, dressed like a student, he held open the door.

'Please,' said Gisevius.

'You have a chauffeur?'

'Are you my chauffeur, Reiner?' Gisevius called.

Reiner smiled widely and said nothing. Gisevius and I climbed into the back of the car and we drove off.

'Where is the office?'

'It is not far. How is my niece?'

'She is well. She sends her love.'

'Of course.'

'Have you any message for her?'

Gisevius turned and smiled. Reiner laughed.

'Tell her – tell her to be good,' said Gisevius. Reiner was beside himself. With a jolt we turned in through an archway and into a small courtyard. The windows on the ground floor were blacked out. Reiner climbed out and closed the gate behind us. I saw him swing a bunch of keys before returning them to his pocket.

'Where are we?' I asked.

'Here is the office,' said Gisevius. Reiner opened the door and gestured me out. There were six storeys of blackened brick and blacked out windows. The sky seemed a long way off and full of snow.

We went through a goods entrance with rubber doors and into a freight lift.

'This isn't the university, is it?' I asked.

Reiner slammed the safety gate shut. Gisevius looked at me with a tolerant smile.

'We must work with what we have,' he said.

We stopped at the top floor. Reiner opened the gate and ushered me into the dim corridor.

'What is going to happen?' I asked.

'Capitalism will in time fail,' said Gisevius. Reiner brought up the rear.

'I mean –'

'My office,' said Gisevius, indicating a glass-panelled door lit from within. The painted lettering on the glass read *Oskar Gisevius: Privatdetektiv*. 'After you, Herr Doktor.' I turned and looked at Reiner, who shrugged good-humouredly and glanced back towards the lift before shaking his head. 'Please. Time is not long.'

The outer office, its windows black, lit by a desk-lamp, contained a hatstand, a desk, a filing cabinet and an office chair in which Steffi sat filing her nails. She wore a suit from forty years before. Another upright chair faced the desk.

'Steffi.'

'Did you bring the book, Richard?'

'What are you doing here?'

'Take Doktor Joyce's coat, Reiner,' said Gisevius.

Reiner helped me out of my coat, hung it on the hatstand, then pressed me down into the chair.

'Did you bring the book, Richard?' Steffi asked again.

'I don't understand what's happening.'

Gisevius nodded. Reiner opened the filing cabinet and took out a metal toolbox. He placed it on the desk and opened it.

Gisevius looked in the box and thought for a while.

Then he pointed.

'That one.'

Reiner produced a pair of pliers.

'Jesus,' I said.

'The book, Richard,' said Steffi.

'What? It's in my coat pocket. Is this about the book?'

'What else?' asked Gisevius. 'Is there something else?'

'What? No. I mean, I brought the book as requested. As instructed.'

Reiner handed *Kiss Me Deadly* to the Professor. He opened it and sniffed the gutter exultantly.

'Beautiful. You should smell this, Reiner. Original Signet edition. Woodpulp. "Quality Reading for the Millions", yes?' Reiner modestly declined. Steffi wrinkled her nose with distaste.

'So are you finished with the pliers?' I asked.

'Not quite,' said Gisevius, sitting on the edge of the desk. He leaned forward and handed me the book.

'What do you want me to do?'

'Surely that is obvious, Doktor Joyce.' He sat back and folded his arms. Steffi lit a cigarette and stared haughtily at the blacked-out window. Reiner lay on his back, propping his head on his hands.

★

'Enough,' said Professor Gisevius after an hour. He took the book from me and placed it in his pocket. 'You read very well. What do you think, Steffi?' She made a little moue of boredom and produced a powder compact. 'Reiner?'

'Mike Hammer is a revolver,' said Reiner.

'You mean a pistol,' Steffi snapped.

'Entschuldigen,' said Reiner.

'More to the point,' said Gisevius, 'he delivers an immanent critique of the system he purports to sustain. Am I correct?' He looked at me.

'Possibly. I haven't read the whole book.'

'Shame on you.'

'I like the girls also,' said Reiner.

'You mean you like the confusion of sex and violence. You are an animal,' said Steffi without looking at him.

'We are all animals,' said Reiner good-naturedly.

'Speak for yourself,' said Steffi.

'Can I go now?' I asked.

'Possibly,' said Gisevius. 'Steffi, have you the document?'

Steffi slid papers from a file and handed them to the Professor.

'Are you ready to sign?' he asked.

'To sign what?'

'Your confession.'

'But I haven't done anything.'

'In the first place that is not true. You have brought this –' Gisevius brandished the book – 'this filth into the East German Republic.'

I looked at him open-mouthed.

'And in the second, it is irrelevant whether you have or have not done anything. Look around you.'

'You are between a cock and a hard place,' ventured Reiner from the floor.

'Will you for God's sake be quiet?' Steffi barked.

'You are pretending to be a private dick,' I said. 'And Steffi is...pretending to be a floozy. And Reiner is a gimp.'

'You are droll, Doktor,' said Reiner, from the floor.

'Sign in the two places indicated,' Gisevius went on, smoothly.

'This is not real. You are playing at – at all this. This fantasy of crime and detection and *film noir*.'

'You have merely to sign.'

'Or what? What is your authority?' I asked. 'You could be anyone.'

'Worry about the fact that I am not, that I am I, Gisevius. Reiner, you will need after all the pliers.'

121

'This part I enjoy also,' said Reiner, lumbering to his feet.

'Hang on,' I said. 'Have you a pen?'

'Of course. It is one of your English pens – an Osmiroid.'

I signed in two places. Reiner returned to the filing cabinet, put away the toolbox and produced a bottle of Schnapps and some shot-glasses.

'A toast: to our fraternal co-operation,' said Reiner.

'To international Socialism,' said Gisevius.

'To us,' I said, looking at Steffi. She gave me a small smile, then came and sat on my knee.

★

I missed my plane home because I spent the night in the doorway of the apartment block in Kreutzberg waiting for Steffi to arrive. Best to travel separately, she said. There was much to explain. This she would do when we were reunited. At six a.m Irmgard approached on foot.

'Where's Steffi?' I asked.

Irmgard shrugged and opened the front door. She would have closed it on me but I pushed in after her.

'Irmgard, where is Steffi?'

'Isn't she with you?'

'Don't fuck about.'

'Very well. I don't know where she is. You can go now. Back to England, yes?'

The lift arrived. Again I pushed in after her.

'This is futile,' said Irmgard.

'I want to see for myself.'

Irmgard shook her head wearily. When we reached the flat she unlocked the door and gestured to me to go ahead. It was not quite light yet but I could see that the living room was empty. I went out on to the balcony. The pool had been drained. In it lay a recliner cushion and a pair of pink goggles.

In the middle distance the Funkturm glittered in the dawn, pumping its cheery drivel into the homes of Actually Existing Socialists in the city next door.

When I went back into the living room Irmgard was sitting on the settee with a young blonde girl in a grubby t-shirt. She lay with her head in Irmgard's lap. They were watching the early news with the sound off.

'Who's this?'

Irmgard did not look up. I repeated the question.

'This is my cousin Annaliese on a visit from the farm where she lives with her grandparents and tends to her pigs and geese. In other words, Richard, fuck off and mind your own business. No, I do not know where Steffi is. And if I did I would not tell you. And if you do not leave now I will call the police. Enjoy your flight.' The blonde girl giggled and stuck out her tongue.

I walked along the wall until I found a viewing platform. From there I stared across the death strip at the blocks of 1960s flats, each with its red and black GDR flag on the balcony awaiting the May Day celebrations. Everything was in order.

When I got home, I waited. After a time I forgot I was waiting. I almost forgot Steffi for a while.

My career as an agent of the GDR failed to flower. I have never found out if anyone in the West even noticed my recruitment to the cause when the Stasi's papers were opened for scrutiny. No one has been in touch. Not our side, not their side. I flatter myself that I was one of the last to be caught in a honeytrap, though it is galling that no one seems to care. I was to supply details of the political tendencies of fellow academics and poets, and of students, in exchange for not being exposed to the British authorities, and I would get to go on sleeping with Steffi with or without her 1940s costume.

What happened? We know what happened. The GDR collapsed. Gysi and the reforming wing of the SED were pushed aside in the rush to change and then to unity. And now there are Nazis all over the former East Germany and the Bundesrepublik is bankrupt. *Plus ca change.* People say they knew the Berlin wall was going to come down. They knew fuck all. They knew no more than me, and I knew *less* than fuck all – I, the agent, actual or imaginary, of a foreign power. Dignity demands that I be right in this regard at least. Who could bear to be the mere patsy of the degenerate phase of what is no-longer-historically-significant?

And now? Let's face it, who reads Mickey Spillane nowadays? Except a few freaks on eBay. As it happens, I've been acquiring original Spillanes for a while. They're quite interesting, in their way. This April I'm taking my stock to a collectors' event being held somewhere in Mitte. You never know. It might be Gisevius. Just. It might be Reiner, bloated with bonhomie. Not Steffi, of course not, but if it is you, then, Liebchen, kiss me deadly.

Not in Gateshead
Any More

The inspectors were removing a fare-dodger from the Metro. She was a feral blonde of forty-odd. She was drunk and didn't want to go. She'd been on when Suzanne boarded in Felling. They were at Jesmond now. Her boyfriend, if that was what he was, a shrivelled creature in a Newcastle shirt, watched in torpor, stretched across the double seat. He was on the brink of making a point, but he couldn't quite reach it. He did have a ticket, it seemed.

'Lorraine, can you not see?' he kept saying, then sliding back to the horizontal. Two polis had arrived now to assist the inspectors. The woman was screaming that she wouldn't go without Dessie.

'Never mind Dessie now,' said the polisman.

Lorraine was hanging on to the pole with one hand. The polis had hold of her legs. You could see her knickers where the denim skirt had ridden up. The rest of the passengers were watching expressionlessly. They knew it could get nasty. You could get sucked in and dragged down somehow if you looked at someone wrong. You could never tell with charvers, or the polis.

Eventually the female copper chopped at Lorraine's forearm with her stick. Lorraine let go of the pole and fell howling to the floor and was bundled on to the platform, shrieking fit to break the windows. Dessie got up slowly and made a guess at the whereabouts of the doors. He was wrong and bashed into a partition. The doors closed and the train pulled out. He shrugged and turned back.

'Aye,' Dessie said. 'What can you fockin dee? Tell me that, aye.' Then, more loudly: 'Worra ye fockin lookin at pal? There but for the fockin grace of God, pal. I tell ye that fer nowt.'

His words followed Suzanne onto the dark platform. It was raining. She pulled up her hood, then took the underpass to the other side of the tracks. The greying white tiles and the urine-smell were like an advert for disappointment. She and Teddy could have ended up like that pair on the Metro, she thought – well, not quite, but hopeless like that, trapped with weakness and endless arguments and getting older. Still, maybe things were looking up. Whatever happened, she was going to the party.

Teddy hadn't liked her taking the job in the library, but she was bored with the council offices in Gateshead. She had a degree. 'Oh, aye,' he'd say. 'Course you have.' As if she hadn't. She thought at first it was the funny hours at the library he minded, with her sometimes having to stay on for an event. But after a while she realised it had to do with her being around all those books. They made Teddy uncomfortable, not that he'd ever come in the door of that library or any other. The idea was enough.

'What d'ye wanna dee that for? I never had ye down for a snob. Anyyroad, what kind of library do people pay to bliddy join? Bliddy daft.'

Teddy was a bathroom fitter. He read *The Daily Star* and followed United. He and his mates went in those bars with topless dancers on match day. He lived in hope of beating seven shades out of a paedophile, but a Mackem would do. He was Toon Army. She used to wonder why he wasn't Gateshead Army, but she'd never liked to ask about that, or much else.

She'd been with him since school. She'd hoped that they could change together. When she did her degree, he more or less put up with it, so she thought maybe he could do — well, something else, she didn't know what. But he didn't want to, so. She started working in administration. They had the flat, the work was steady, the money OK, but.

'So what's your problem? Am ah not good enough any more?'

'We want different things, Teddy.'

'Ah don't. I want the same, me. And ye? Ye divvint kna what yer want. Never fockin happy. Books aren't real. Neither are the snobs that read them. It's a con — these writers are parasites.' The same hopeless argument, endlessly. It was easier to pour a glass of wine. Maybe the woman on the metro had got started like that, ending up welded to a nomark.

She'd always liked writing stories at school, and lately she'd felt the impulse to start writing again. She did a bit in secret when Teddy was out. It cost her a lot of nerve, but she showed a few pages to Maureen, a colleague in the library. Maureen was older and probably spent all her evenings reading.

'Not bad,' said Maureen. 'So your heroine gets a demon lover, eh? Builds up quite an atmosphere. What are you going to do with it?'

'How d'you mean?'

'I mean it's quite good, Suzanne. Mebbes you could tidy it up a bit.'

'What for?'

'Well, to publish, or something.'

'Nah! You're joking.'

'Well, you never know. Or you could do a course. Creative Writing. You should.'

Teddy would never stand for that.

'Me? No way.'

Maureen shrugged, but she handed Suzanne a leaflet for a competition that had just come in. For tales of the supernatural. The best entries would be published in an anthology. She'd never heard of either of the judges, but what did she know?

She had an idea for a new story, but she wasn't sure how much of one it was. She worked on it when Teddy was out. Normally there was only him used the computer, for playing online poker. She called the story 'Not in Gateshead Any More.' It was about a girl who found she had a double and… well, they changed places by meeting in the middle of the Tyne Bridge, so the first girl took over the second girl's life and vice versa, except the second girl did what the first girl secretly wanted - she did her no good useless jealous feller in, but the first girl got away with it because she was over on this side now, and not in Gateshead, so the rules didn't apply. It sounded daft when you summed it up. Anyway.

Working on the computer, Suzanne also discovered, incidentally, that Teddy was corresponding via a chatroom with a Wallsend woman called Pinkie. Pinkie described herself as an old-fashioned girl, except in bed. Suzanne could well imagine. She worked on her story with a will after that. But it was still very difficult to put the envelope in the post. What if something happened?

She came third. That was a hundred pounds. And she would be in the book. But who could she tell? Her Dad was dead and her Mam was no good at new things – they worried her. She would just ask why Suzanne and Teddy didn't get wed. For the first time ever, she told Teddy a direct lie. She said she had to work late. He didn't like it, but he said he'd be at the match anyway that night.

There was quite a crowd. They had drinks near the big table in the main library, with Hazel serving, dressed up as a Victorian widow in black bombazine. Suzanne drank a couple of glasses too quickly, to try to settle her nerves. Then they were going over the covered bridge and through the Mining Institute Library to reach the lecture theatre downstairs. She was carried along in the chatting crowd. Maureen gave her an encouraging smile.

The lecture theatre was wood-panelled and ornately

corniced, with steep wooden steps and deep scarlet leather cushions on the benches. All around the walls were pictures of old men with beards looking satisfied. She was shown to a seat at the front. Nervousness and the drink made her hot, and her thoughts wandered off.

Then she found the announcements had begun without her noticing. Someone nudged her, and she was on her feet, going forward to read her story. She got through it somehow. People clapped while she shook hands with the judges, then she was given an envelope and the book. She sat down again, feeling cherry-red but very pleased. She'd never won anything until now, not even the meat draw in the local. It was impossible to concentrate on the other stories.

At the end a man with a camera appeared smiling in front of her and got her to join the judges and the other winners. He took several pictures. A young woman with a notepad asked her some questions. Suzanne forgot everything she said as soon as it was out of her mouth.

Then a crowd of them were out in the crisp late autumn air. The stars glittered fiercely over the Keep as they approached the pub. Across the river far below, the lights of Gateshead glittered too. She wondered for a moment where Teddy was, but the glassy roar of the packed bar took over and she was ushered to a bay seat and given a large glass of red wine. The prizewinners toasted each other. She felt warm and elated and not drunk, not really.

She hadn't taken in the judges before, but now Maureen, who seemed to know everyone, introduced her properly. Russell was the tall man, forty-odd, very smiley, with stubble and a black hat that made him look like a Serbian warlord. He wrote fantasy novels and kept cats. Beverley was mebbes a bit younger, dark, a bit like if your auntie was a witch but nice.

'Enjoyed it lots,' said Russell. 'Good villain, I thought. Nasty little man.'

'Nice touch, using the bridge,' said Beverley. 'Good

structure.'

'As it were,' said Russell. 'Have you got lots of stories?'

'Me? Nah,' said Suzanne. 'Only a couple.'

'Then you should write some more immediately,' said Beverley, crisply. They both sounded a bit posh, but it didn't seem to matter. They were proper writers. Under the table Suzanne flicked through the competition anthology to find herself. There she was, Suzanne Scott: author and real person. 'And make sure,' Beverley added, 'that you never forget the value of surprise.'

Maureen handed Suzanne another leaflet, for a writing course at one of the universities. Entry level. Beverley and Russell were the tutors. The fee made her blink, but she could manage it. Then the others were talking about books and writers they knew, some that she'd heard of, and gossiping, and she felt the naughty addictive excitement of it, and the warm red glow expanded to take her in completely.

★

'You told me you were working,' said Teddy, waving the *Chronicle* at her. She said nothing but went on stirring the beans. Her head still hurt from last night's wine. 'Writing?' he persisted. 'What have *ye* got to write about?'

'Just a bit of fun.'

'Look at these wankers.' He pointed at Russell and Beverley in the photo.

'The judges. Published writers.'

'Writers, oh, aye. They've got you talking about your next story here,' he said. 'You're not a writer.' He slapped the photograph for emphasis.

'Don't tear it. I might be.'

'I might be Alan bloody Shearer. But am not, am ah?'

'I can't see why you're that bothered. If I enjoy writing and that, where's the harm? You've got your interests.'

'Football's not a fockin interest. It's football! Anway,' he went on, 'you're finished with your writing and with that bloody library. Get back to the council. Or Nettos. I don't care which.'

'So that's you telling me, is it?'

'Aye.' The air crackled dangerously.

'I see. So what does Pinkie do for a living then? Is she on the tills?' Suzanne felt furious and madly emboldened. 'Or just on the game?'

Teddy grabbed her by the chin with one hand and pinched her nose with the other. The beans spilt over the cooker.

'Now ye listen,' he spat. 'Dee as yer telt and keep yer neb out of me bits of things. That's private – nowt to dee with yee. Yer reckon yer a clever cow, see if ye can follow these simple instructions.'

He hauled her up to the spare bedroom, sat her down at the computer and made her wipe the story. Then he told her to go and clean up and get the dinner on again. He took the anthology away too. He had never laid hands on her before. She was shaking with anger and fear, but she had the computer memory stick hidden in a drawer.

After the weekend she told him she'd handed in her notice but that the library needed three months. Now he didn't seem that bothered. He just grunted and went out. She checked his internet records; easy to figure out his password: FC1969 – Fairs Cup, and the last time the Toon had won anything. Even she knew that.

Pinkie was still on the go in the chatroom. Very keen. She'd posted a photo. She was agile, you had to give her that. Suzanne found she didn't care. The problem was, Teddy would never let her go, whatever he got up to himself. So it didn't matter that she'd lied again. She hadn't put her notice in. What she needed was time to think. There must be a way out.

Maureen asked her if she wanted to go to a writers' group. It was on a Saturday afternoon, so Suzanne told Teddy she was going shopping. He was off to the Boro anyway, to watch the match. The address was in the West End. Turned out it was Russell's place, an old wide-fronted villa near the Moor. The huge living room was completely stuffed with books and DVDs, the stairs were covered in more piles and the hallway was full of new arrivals waiting for a place. As far as she could tell, for Russell everything else except cooking and cats – she couldn't count all the cats - came second to words and images. He kept his hat on all the time, she noticed. Maureen was there, and Beverley, and a younger couple dressed as Goths. Everyone seemed to wear black.

The idea was that you read a few pages and then people commented. This made her very nervous, but everyone was drinking wine, and the stories were interesting but not all that much better than hers, she thought, and when it was her turn she read a bit of 'Not in Gateshead Any More' and everyone seemed to enjoy it. So when Russell and Beverley made a few points about ways she could improve the story, it felt helpful rather than negative. There was a card for her, inviting her to a party at Beverley's on Friday. She said yes, but God knew how she'd get there.

It was already dark when they finished. She was on her way to the bus stop when Teddy got out of the car in front of her.

'I fockin telt ye,' he hissed.

'I thought you were in the Boro,' was all she could think of to say.

'I knaa ye did. But there's nae fixture this week, is there?' He grabbed her by the arm and dragged her back to Russell's front door, where he leaned on the bell.

'I'm sorry, Russell –' she said as the door opened.

Teddy pushed her to the pavement and dragged Russell out into the street, pinning him against the railings.

'There's no need for this,' said Russell, mildly. Teddy slapped him round the head. Russell's hat fell on the ground.

'Ah'll tell ye onny once, pal. You and your crowd of fockin parasites are gonna leave wor lass' – he pointed – 'alone, understand. I knaa your sort – feeding on the weak-minded cos ye cannot bear to dee a decent day's work yerselves. She doesn't need ye and yer shite, OK?' Teddy slapped Russell round the head again. 'Cos she's got me. Understand?'

'I can hear what you're saying.'

'I fockin hope so, otherwise I'll be back to set fire to your house, and ye and yer fockin books with it.' Teddy let go of Russell, who picked up his hat and dusted it off, looking carefully at Teddy, who had now turned to Suzanne. 'Now get in the fockin car and divvint say a word.'

★

A couple of nights later, Teddy didn't come home after work. She thought nothing of it. He'd stayed in a foul mood, roaring and swearing about fockin parasites and snobs. A second night passed, and still he didn't show up. She rang him and kept getting voicemail. She rang his Mam.

'I'm not surprised, the way ye've tret the poor lad,' said Teddy's Mam.

They hadn't seen him at work either. She called the police, who were pretty unenthusiastic because it was so soon and clearly a domestic and, as Suzanne had felt obliged to tell them, there was mebbes another woman mixed up in it.

Christmas was on its way. She was uncertain what to do. Mebbes he'd cut his losses and hooked up with Pinkie. They were probably made for each other. She felt angry, then empty, then free. She studied the party invitation. Still time if she got a move on.

Forgetting the sad couple on the Metro, Suzanne pressed the doorbell of Beverley's house. Beverley answered, looking very glam in black and silver. There were already quite a few people there – some she recognised from the writers' group, others she was introduced to, all a bit Goth, but friendly and all getting stuck into the plentiful red wine and the table loaded with various meats and cheeses. Beverley was coming to and fro from the kitchen all the time, so Suzanne asked if she needed any help.

'This lot will drink the sea dry, so we need reinforcements. Could you bring another case up from the cellar? It's the door under the stairs.'

Suzanne found she wanted to hug herself with happiness. Bugger Teddy. She switched on the light and went down into the chill of the cellar. There was one wall made up of wine racks, all full, plus cases of wine on the floor, and a big chest freezer. This must be what it was like being a writer.

Suzanne couldn't have said why, but suddenly she took a notion to ring Teddy again. She hoped he'd answer, so she could tell him where she was and who with and how she didn't care. There was probably no signal down here, but sod it anyway.

She hit the speed-dial. There was a pause, and then she heard Teddy's phone ring out. A moment later a phone rang somewhere nearby. It went on ringing, She looked around. Someone must have left a mobile down here, but where? She rang off and the ringing in the cellar stopped.

She began to feel a bit strange. She called the number again; the ringing began once more. Where? She moved towards the freezer. It seemed louder over here. Almost laughing with bemusement, she lifted the freezer's lid. Inside lay Teddy, stark naked, frosty, the colour of whitewash, his phone blinking in one frozen hand. The voicemail sounded in her own phone. She raised it to her ear.

'This is Teddy. Leave a message. I'm not here.'

Piled at Teddy's feet were large clear containers of what she thought must be blood.

There were footsteps behind her. Russell and Beverley stood shyly at the foot of the stairs, smiling. The other guests crowded down behind them.

'Exsanguination, they call it. Lovely black pudding, eventually,' said Russell.

'Teddy was right,' said Beverley. 'We *are* all parasites, aren't we?' The others nodded and laughed politely. 'You're not in Gateshead any more, Suzanne.'

In the Silence Room

Situated one floor beneath the main library, the Silence Room remains what it always was, a chamber set apart for strictly undisturbed study. It is a dim place, large, high-ceilinged like the rest of the building. It contains tall stacks of county records and suchlike. There are small desks between the stacks, with a larger, much-coveted table at the far end. The parquet floor is part-covered by an ancient carpet, while the quality of light in the room resembles diluted beef tea, matching both panelling and wallpaper. It is never bright; the sun does not enter directly. But there are plenty of lamps and it is quiet: the incontinent chunterers from the big table upstairs never descend this far. As a place of work it has much to recommend it.

But people in general, including the staff, do not like the Silence Room. This is not a view they will volunteer, and if prompted to account for it they will be vexingly unspecific: it is, you see, a *feeling*, of a kind they might find difficult to describe even to themselves. For the actual origins of this collective unease have been forgotten. An alienist might say they have been repressed.

The beginning of this tale is simply told. In the last years of the long peace before the outbreak of the Great War, the conflict which was to kill so many of the scholars and writers and idlers who made the library their second and perhaps their true home, there were two poets, Ralph Exton and James McGrain, long-standing members of the library, committee members from time to time, who on the brink of middle life engaged in a quarrel which destroyed what had until then been a close literary friendship. The subject of the quarrel was the future of poetry – a fit subject for dispute at any time, certainly, but in this case unfortunate in the destructive passions it evoked. Not to labour literary matters, Exton stood firmly in the English romantic tradition and was somewhat akin to De La Mare, while McGrain saw modernity in the offing and was anxious to embrace its transforming artistic possibilities. He had caught the scent of Ezra Pound from afar.

For Exton, poetry was an aspect of belief, a means of ingress to the Mysteries, to be sought in and from any direction that suggested itself – Europe, the East, Christian sources or others – Hermetic, Sufic, Zoroastrian, all these and more had their possibilities. The world was a surface which it was the poet's task to penetrate in order to encounter and report on what lay beyond. Exton's enthusiasms, then, were eclectic and it would be fair to say that they inclined to be more energetic than precise.

If in Exton's view there were more things in Heaven and Earth than McGrain had dreamed of, to the Scot it seemed that there were actually quite enough to be going on with. His view was altogether more sceptical and rigorous. He was a dry soul, perhaps, though he might not have agreed to having a soul at all. Some people understandably asked why it had taken so long for him to lose patience with his friend's indulgent attitudes. It would be sad, but not unreasonable, to suggest that the dispute was indirectly connected with the news that an inaugural Chair of Literature was to be instituted at the College. This would mark a significant development in the importance and autonomy of the institution. It need hardly be said that it would also represent an important step in the career of the scholar appointed to the post; it would of course be equally redundant to remark that neither Exton nor McGrain would have considered engaging in direct competition, for they were in the first place gentlemen. Exton, be it added, was the more likely to succeed to the post, for his eccentricities of taste were not unfamiliar. McGrain, on the other hand, for all his sound scholarship, was felt to have a slightly metallic air of *newness* about him.

While such disputes are perhaps essential to the health of literature, it is, sadly, in their nature to induce permanent schism and bitterness and to provoke others to take sides. Though the two men had been acquainted since Ralph Exton had come down from Oxford and James McGrain from Edinburgh to teach in the institution which was later to become Kings College, and though the two were linked through a multitude of shared literary preoccupations, and even though McGrain had married Ralph's cousin, when the quarrel broke out the two cut off all relations. The gulf between them became so wide and deep that it seemed to exceed any possibility of being bridged, though the wives, Marianne McGrain and Isabel Exton, maintained discreet contact and shared the view that it was all a storm in a teacup, which may have been true but was of little help to those who found themselves tempest-tossed in the teacup in question.

In itself, this quarrel could scarcely make a story. A footnote, perhaps, in the relevant history. Neither poet's work has survived the winnowing of the years, though all of it may still be consulted by the curious in the upper gallery of the library. What is more intriguing is the turn which events now took: one December day Ralph Exton disappeared from the face of the earth. He entered the library as usual after lunch, following his lecture at the college. He greeted the staff at the issue desk, then asked for the gas to be lit in the Silence Room. Stennett, the caretaker on duty, accompanied Exton downstairs, lit the lamps as requested and left Exton laying out his papers on the large table. There was still a faint autumn light from the windows, which looked out across a tiny alleyway on to the sooty walls of the Coroner's Court. Stennett was sure that there was no one else present. Having asked if the Doctor required any further assistance, Stennett returned to the kitchen-cubbyhole at the top of the stairs and resumed his conversation with Mrs Crashaw at the tea urn. Dr Exton, he said later, had seemed much as usual, polite but preoccupied and clearly anxious to get on with his work. As to the nature of that work on the day in question, Stennett, a reader of the popular prints, did not feel competent to say, although his eye had been caught by an ink drawing of a rectangular patterned surface of enormously intricate design, to which the doctor was beginning to give his attention when the caretaker left. It was, as Stennett averred, none of his business what the gentleman chose to do with his time.

Exton's disappearance was met then and later with complete bafflement. The local press, conscious of serving a maritime city, attempted unsatisfactory comparisons with the disappearance of the crew of the *Marie Celeste* some forty years before. The public rooms at the other end of the corridor on that floor were sealed off for redecoration at the time of the disappearance, which meant that the only way out was to return by the stairs, up past the kitchen, where Mrs Crashaw made it a point of honour to observe all those who came and went and if possible engage them in conversation. She would not have missed Dr Exton if he had come past. What Stennett chose to tell only the librarian, who told only the police, who later told McGrain, was that the Silence Room had been locked from the inside. In the room itself, Exton's overcoat was still on a hook by the door, while his papers lay spread out on the table – poems, notes, a draft of an essay on the minor Romantic poet Thomas Lovell Beddoes, and among these things the ink drawing which Stennett had noticed earlier, to which had been hastily added a few lines of verse.

The police found nothing to go on. The windows had long been painted shut and it was clear that no one had touched them in some time. The investigating officer Sergeant March's only recourse was to interrogate McGrain in the faint hope that he would reveal that the poets' quarrel had taken a homicidal and tragic turn, and that he had somehow spirited away Exton's corpse and disposed of it while contriving to seal the door.

Naturally, this line of enquiry led nowhere. For one thing, McGrain (by now unanimously appointed to the Chair of Literature) was clearly deeply troubled by the disappearance of his erstwhile friend. He was particularly disturbed by what seemed to him the likelihood that Exton had realised that his position in their argument was in the last analysis indefensible and had therefore, like many another before him, succumbed to literary despair and gone off secretly to take his own life. The river might simply be slow in yielding its secrets in this case. In entertaining such a proposition McGrain might be thought to have revealed a failure to grasp the tenacity of literary vanity in others, not to mention himself.

In time Exton's papers were returned to his grieving widow, and the attention of the press and the authorities moved on. Sergeant March had no choice but to file the material and try to forget it, though he gave Mrs March to understand that in the matter of Dr Exton there was some sleight, some stratagem, something somehow disrespectful of the rules of criminal investigation, and that the Sergeant was pretty sure he had been cheated somehow, perhaps – here he gave a significant look - in an oriental manner.

Soon the war came and swept away the world to which Exton had belonged. As a reservist called to the colours, McGrain saw service in the Intelligence Corps in Mesopotamia and returned with an MC, a stiff right leg and a working knowledge of several Middle Eastern languages. But his duty was not yet done, for in the days of their friendship the two poets had appointed each other executors of their respective estates. When after seven years Exton was declared dead and his will was examined, he turned out not to have altered this provision.

'There,' said Marianne McGrain, 'you see – it would

only have been a matter of time and your friendship would have been restored.'

'There speaks your kind heart, my darling. I think it far more likely that Exton had too much to concern him to think of amending his will.'

'And have you changed yours?' asked Marianne, suppressing her irritation.

'I have not. And my reasons are the same as those of Exton. I have been too busy with the college and my own work. Besides, I hope – as Exton must have hoped - not to trouble the undertaker for some little time yet.'

'Well, you must alter your will now.'

'I shall ask Groves to take on the executorship of my work. He's a publisher for one thing. For another, he's young.'

'Poor Ralph was barely thirty-five. And Isobel and the children have so little to live on. You must do what you can for them as executor.'

'I shall, my dear. Of course I shall.'

And do he did. McGrain oversaw the publication of Exton's final book of poems, *The Moon and the Forest*, and then began the work of collating and assembling the materials which would form Exton's *Collected Poems* and the *Collected Essays*. It was the least McGrain could do, though it stuck in his craw to spend his time on poems he considered fustily outmoded and sentimental, the death throes of a tradition exhausted forty years before. Why had Exton not been able to see the facts and move on? Yet if he could not assent to Exton's sensibility, nonetheless McGrain acknowledged the passion and the care with which Exton kept faith with the gone world of faery lands forlorn and with the brisker eroticism of Byron. These days McGrain could scarcely read Keats or the wicked milord without wanting to wash his hands. But he allowed no liberties to his resentment as he worked his way through his vanished friend's literary remains.

In fact the item which particularly piqued McGrain's curiosity was the drawing or diagram to which Stennett had referred. McGrain repeatedly returned to this sheet of unlined foolscap. On it Exton had drawn a rectangular surface, intricately and minutely patterned, as Sennett had said. There was a sense of order in the drawing that reminded McGrain of Islamic art, an order both unforgiving and intoxicating, as though – it struck him; he dismissed it – mathematics had been turned into desire. At the same time, despite himself – he may have been a poet, but he didn't like to let things run away with him – he acknowledged a sense of disquiet and anxiety in the image. It was also familiar. But from where? Next to the drawing a single quatrain had been written, seemingly in haste, in what McGrain recognised as Exton's handwriting. The verse said:

> *Let no one take this dancing floor*
> *Who dreams he may return,*
> *But whisper now this verse three times*
> *To find what you would learn.*

It seemed to McGrain that this was merely a late, fugitive example of the slackly mysterious manner which had come to infect Exton's work in later years. There was altogether too much twilight and important vagueness in it for McGrain's taste. Yet McGrain acknowledged the poignancy of finding this, perhaps Exton's final utterance, in these circumstances. Marianne agreed.

'It is as though poor Ralph knew his time was short,' she said.

'Did Isobel perhaps mention that Ralph was worried about his health?'

'Never. She said he was simply pressing on with his work as keenly as always.'

'But what was he working on in particular?'

'He was as private with her as with everybody else on

that matter. As are you, I might add.'

'Quite.'

McGrain could not have said why that afternoon he decided to go and work in the Silence Room. He took the drawing in his briefcase with others of Exton's papers. There was nothing superstitious about him. He did not share the discreet unease of the staff about being in the room where Exton had disappeared. He drew a distinction: Exton had gone, but surely he had not *vanished*. The river had provided no answer, but there would be an explanation somewhere, at some time, if somebody cared to find it, however unlikely it might seem. For the present, McGrain had more than enough work to be getting on with.

He had been reading Exton's extensive journals, not because he expected them to find publication but in case they might provide some clue to the poet's rather melodramatic disappearance. Now he turned to the final entry, dated 11th December, the day on which the poet had apparently been seen for the last time. It read:

'How long I had secretly despaired at the disenchantment of the world and its contents only I can know. - Despaired that the charge formerly carried by everyday objects is now lost to them, or to me. Had I been wrong or was time stealing my power to see into the life of things? Far greater poets than I could ever hope to be have suffered the same sense that the world had closed its gates to them, or worse, that it had died. At times I have even wondered if my lost friend McGrain is correct in his barren, stony positivism. Dark days, indeed. But the solution lay before me if I cared to look, in this very room, ignored, forgotten, sleeping. And now I look.'

McGrain smiled in puzzlement and looked from these words to the drawing and its accompanying verse. Had Exton been indulging in opiates, perhaps? What on earth could the Silence Room offer him to relieve his despondency? Sourly amused, McGrain began a slow circuit of the stacks in case a clue should present itself. Preoccupied and irritated, he tripped on the slightly raised corner of the carpet. For a little while he remained on his knees, staring at the half-obliterated design. If this carpet were cleaned now, it might well disintegrate. Why had no one thrown the thing away? Then, with a start, he rose and went to the desk. He picked up the drawing and went back to stand in the middle of the carpet. The pattern was faintly discernible under the decades of dirt. Exton had been *sketching the carpet* – the act surely, of a man in the grip of utter boredom with himself, and perhaps on the brink of derangement. McGrain laughed aloud, shaking his head – at which point Stennett came into the room.

'Is something wrong, Dr McGrain?' Stennett asked, looking about suspiciously as though McGrain might have a hidden companion with him.

'No, Stennett. There is no need to concern yourself. I was simply amused, so I laughed. I promise to keep silence from now on.'

'As you wish, sir.' Stennett made to go, then turned and added, 'It was just that Dr Exton was in the habit of laughing somewhat the same when he was down in here, towards the end. It was not what you might call a *comfortable* noise, sir. It was odd to hear it again. And that's why I came in.' Stennett showed no sign of moving.

'Since you're here, Stennett, perhaps you can answer a question for me,' said McGrain.

'I will certainly try, sir,' said Stennett, cautiously.

'This carpet.'

'Carpet. Yes sir. Should have been taken out and burnt long since. Only we can't.'

'Why ever not?'

'It's Colonel Severance's Turkish, sir. He brought it back

from his, erm, adventures in those parts. And he donated it to the library, along with all his papers, so we can hardly get rid of it, even though someone will likely break their neck tripping on that corner.'

'I nearly did so myself,' said McGrain.

'Exactly, sir.' Stennett himself seemed disinclined to set foot on the carpet at all. 'It's either too big or too small – thirteen by thirteen: I've measured it.'

'Really.' McGrain looked down again at the dull carpet and trod on the raised corner – to no avail; it resumed its position, somewhat, it seemed to him, like a curled lip. 'Colonel Severance, you say?'

'Gone to meet his Maker long since, sir. He was an old gentleman when I was taken on as a lad. Dead these forty years. Shame he didn't take his bloody carpet with him, begging your pardon, sir.'

When Stennett had gone away again, McGrain set about comparing the drawing to the carpet. The deep reds and blues and ochres seemed more clearly visible beneath the muck now – partly, he supposed, because he was paying proper attention, partly because he now knew what he was looking at. It was odd how the abstraction of the pattern – the central spiral answered at the corners, the balance of squares and rectangles occupying the remainder – it was odd how it seemed to evoke distance, dry air, heat, even a dry sea.

Time was getting on. Marianne would be expecting him home; they were to go out to a concert. But he lingered, looking, comparing. Then he went to the door, opened it and looked about in the hallway in case Stennett was still in the offing. As he turned to re-enter the room, he saw with a smile that Stennett, perhaps distracted by their conversation, seemed to have left his key on the outside of the lock. McGrain looked at his watch and put it away. No one need know of this private frivolity. It would not take long. He removed the key, re-entered the room and with a smile of boyish glee quietly locked the door and put the key in his pocket. This done, he returned to the desk, picked up the drawing and with an exaggerated movement stepped on to the carpet.

'Speak the verse, I pray you, trippingly,' he said, quietly so that if Stennett were still nearby he would not hear.

He felt curiously exposed, standing there. He looked again at the verse and began to read:

> *'Let no one take this dancing floor*
> *Who dreams he may return,*
> *But whisper now this verse three times*
> *To find what you would learn.'*

The silence settled back as if he had never spoken. McGrain was glad he was alone, for he felt foolish now. His mouth was a little dry.

He continued:

> *'Let no one take this dancing floor*
> *Who dreams he may return,*
> *But whisper now this verse three times*
> *To find what you would learn.'*

Again, nothing. But what had he been expecting? No one must ever find out about this undignified folly. But he read on into the silence:

> *'Let no one take this dancing floor*
> *Who dreams he may return,*
> *But whisper now this verse three times*
> *To find what you would learn.'*

Nothing.

Or, no – had the silence somehow become a kind of waiting in itself? A minute passed. Another. Nothing. That was quite enough of that, he thought. Time he was off. But then, before McGrain could move, and almost as though in response to his intention to do so, the far, raised corner of the carpet slowly rose a little further, as though on a breeze, then sank back.

McGrain watched, transfixed. After a few moments the corner rose again, a little higher this time, and a low ripple ran through the carpet towards him on a diagonal. He felt it flow under his feet and made to step back but found he could not. A further ripple came, more strongly now, followed by a low wave passing through the material, while the edge of the carpet behind him rose and fell as though it were surf breaking on a shore. McGrain became afraid.

When he looked back across the carpet he found that the far corner had risen, like a hood, to waist-height. The next wave made McGrain stumble. To his horror, his hands seemed to sink through the surface as though – impossible, he thought - through dry water. He saw the drawing lying on the floor and thought that if he could reach it he might somehow undo this – this what? – this dreadful hallucination. But the next wave broke over his head and for a moment he sank into a baking darkness. When he broke surface he could feel nothing underfoot. He lay thrashing and choking among the re-awoken colours, the crimson and fierce blues and parched ochres that seemed now to be passing over and through him. And now the fringed hood rose further, slowly approaching across the flashing, coiling surface of the carpet, until it hung above him, seeming to regard him eyelessly. McGrain cried out, but there was no sound, and the hood drew back for an instant before descending in a single muscular, glittering, serpentine wave. In that moment McGrain thought he heard Exton ask him a question: *Now do you believe me?*

Which, ladies and gentlemen, may well be the reason why people in general do not care for the Silence Room, where the carpet is still quietly sleeping even as we speak.

Once Again Assembled Here

'Who can ever praise enough
The world of his belief?'
W.H. Auden, 'The Price'

When the birches shed their leaves you would be able to see
all the way across the school field, over the rugby pitches to
the railway line and the old engine shed, beyond which lay
the allotments and the haze of the city centre. The landscape
was all so intimately, effortlessly known that it was as if he had
always been the possessor of this view, which in turn had
simply waited for him to take up residence and start looking.
Off to the left, the old school stood on its dignity, a vast late-
Victorian ship of state made of dark brick and masonry – a
cross between a belated Oxbridge chapel and a prison, he'd
always thought, with a touch of the madhouse about the
highest windows, those that had no rooms behind them.

Andrews stood and smoked at the open bedroom
window, bored and appalled at the outcome. Below him an
elderly lady made her way home with her shopping. Fernbank
was a cul-de-sac. Amen to that. He had read Auden's lines in
'Letter to Lord Byron' about Rabbitarse and String, but he
had never expected to call on their services in person.
Something had gone wrong somewhere. He had made a mess
of things without even noticing. The results had not been as
he had hoped. The opportunity for further study had gone.
Disappointment had intervened. Alas. And so on. However
many ways he stated the case, he could neither account for it
nor entirely believe it. He had pissed it away: there were the
words, and their meaning was clear, but he could not attach

149

them to his failure.

Now he found himself on the far side of the disaster. And therefore (it felt like a therefore), in the mysterious way by which accident turned into inescapable design, he also found himself accepting a temporary appointment at Blake's. It was all wrong, but there seemed to be nothing to be done except make the best of it. That was a skill Andrews had hoped to grow out of, since it stood too clearly for the grey apologetic demeanour of his entire family, living and dead – a distinction he had come to feel was academic. Never mind, they would say. Never mind. Let nothing happen. But he did mind.

He lit another cigarette and returned to the view. This feeling he was experiencing: what was it? It seemed to be a sense of distant horror, except that the distance was steadily, impassively diminishing. He had declined an invitation to have tea with Mrs Abbott to mark his arrival, claiming he had urgent correspondence to deal with. But now he changed his mind and went downstairs to join her in the back garden. Never mind.

★

Earlier that day he had entered Blake's for the first time in years, by means of a side door the boys were forbidden to use. Naturally it had been a point of honour for them to use it as much as possible. Now that he was permitted to pass through this door, he found he still retained a flicker of anxiety about getting caught. The thing to do was sidle down the dim, green-tiled lower Junior corridor and then nip into the lavatories and out through a further exit into the legitimate thoroughfare which led eventually to the Main Hall. Staff did not enter the lavatories, generally speaking. Tyzack had observed that presumably this was one reason they were all so full of shit. Where was Tyzack now?

Bruckner, the Second Master and Head of History, had

been in his room as usual. This was a breezy corner lair whose windows he forbade anyone to close. On winter afternoons, the room would fill steadily with fog from the rugby pitch outside, while Bruckner, with his exploding eyebrows, his Nazi orchestral conductor's silver mane, and his sudden bouts of exemplary violence, enquired into the causes of the Thirty Years' War.

Andrews smiled thinly and remembered.

'Please sir,' Tyzack had asked one afternoon. 'What became of the Swedes after the death of Gustavus Adolphus at Lutzen?'

'What makes you think it's any of your business, Tyzack, you stinking goblin?' Bruckner replied, baring his teeth.

'Please, sir, the unexamined life is not worth living.'

'I imagine you can devise my next remark for yourself.'

'Yes, sir.'

'What are you?'

'A dolt, sir. A verminous toad.'

Today Andrews had found himself knocking at the half-open door of Bruckner's room. Silence. He went in, telling himself not to be a coward.

'Well, Andrews,' said Bruckner, unaltered, eternal, glaring happily over the battlements of his desk, 'here you are. This is a surprise – at any rate for you. Just when you thought you had shaken our dust from your feet, but never mind. You are joining us to replace Mr Thorne.'

'Temporarily.'

'We shall have to see.'

'For one term.'

'If I were you, Andrews, I should hesitate to make any assumptions. There's a divinity that shapes our ends, as the poet has it. In your case the divinity is Gabbitas-Thring, of course. Which in itself should commend a certain modesty of attitude, no?'

'So where has Mr Thorne gone?' Andrews knew Thorne

from the lower years of his schooling. He taught History and Divinity. He had a vast, egg-shaped head and round, thick, ever-smeary spectacles. Now that Andrews thought of him, the ancient feeling clarified itself: Thorne was a man trying hard to be kind, though it did not come easily to him; he was also a bit creepy, perhaps.

'Mr Thorne? I couldn't accurately say offhand. People come and go, some of them, and in no one place remain,' Bruckner replied, rising from his desk to hand Andrews a heavy blue file. 'Your classes.'

Andrews flicked through the top few sheets.

'It says Divinity here. I don't do Divinity. I'm a historian.'

'Are you?'

'It's what I did at Cambridge.'

'So I see.' Bruckner picked up a piece of paper and displayed it: Andrews's letter of application to Blake's. Evidence for the prosecution. Bruckner folded the paper away. 'Thorne took Divinity. Thorne is not here. Ergo. There will possibly be some English too.'

'There must have been a misunderstanding.'

'I dare say. Chaos besets us at every turn. But here we are. Don't you know there's a war on, Andrews?'

Andrews was baffled for a moment, then decided that Bruckner meant Vietnam.

'No, there isn't. And PE. There's PE down here as well.'

'Mens sana.'

'You must be joking.'

'Has anything in our long and unhappy acquaintance justified such an inference, Andrews? You may go now. We gather to begin term on Monday.'

'Is the Head about?'

'The Head is a busy man. The door, Andrews.'

★

Mrs Abbott, tiny and completely white but for her stern arterial lipstick, led him to the summerhouse where she arranged the tea-things on a rattan table. She already knew he was a Blake's old boy, and seemed to think this lent matters an apt completeness indicative of the care of Providence for small matters. *Lord receive us with thy blessing, / Once again assembled here.* It was still warm but the leaves were turning.

Someone was practising the piano in the house next door. Andrews recognised 'Clair de Lune'. Not bad.

'That's Philippa, the Jemsons' elder daughter,' said Mrs Abbott. 'She's got a place at the Royal Northern College. She's at Dame Clare's, of course. Their sixth-formers come over to take part in the plays at Blake's. But of course you'd know that.'

Andrews would indeed. How could he forget *Macbeth* and the sight of Deirdre Scanlon imploring the powers of darkness to unsex her? Either she had misunderstood the line, Andrews had thought, on all three nights, as he stood in the wings in his Third Murderer's costume, or she was a very dirty girl. The review in *The Blakean* had passed over this aspect of the production, preferring to discuss the lighting, but during a party at Tyzack's house one summer evening Andrews had looked into the matter privately, behind a settee. What had become of Deirdre Scanlon? He remembered that her parents ran a pet shop.

'Fond memories, Mr Andrews?' Mrs Abbott was twinkling at him and holding out a plate. 'Try a macaroon.' Obediently he took one. The music had stopped. After a time Mrs Abbott sighed. 'Of course, Mr Thorne used to like to sit out here on warm evenings and do his marking. We kept each other company, along with Roger.'

'Roger?'

'My old cat. He got run over on the main road. Mr Thorne found him there one night and brought him home. There was nothing anyone could do.'

'No one seems to know what happened to him. Mr

Thorne, I mean.'

'I'm afraid not.' Mrs Abbott produced a pair of secateurs from her cardigan pocket. 'You sit tight, Mr Andrews. Enjoy the sun. The nights are already drawing in. But I dare say we shall make do.'

★

Next came Friday. There should be something festive with which to occupy himself, but all Andrews could imagine was getting drunk. After lunch he slept for a while with a green Penguin Margery Allingham unopened on his chest. Then, struggling to bear his own company, he went out. He took a short cut through the graveyard and down the cut to Queens Avenue beside the mid-terraced house where the hippies had lived in complacent squalor with their dogs and a crusty copy of *Forever Changes*, smoking dope and deflowering schoolgirls. The place was boarded up.

A couple of hundred yards along the street was Smallbone's stamp shop. Andrews paused and looked in the window. There was Smallbone behind the counter, talking to someone not shown.

Andrews went in. The bell rang and Smallbone looked up with suppressed alarm. He must have been sucked back into the family somehow. The last Andrews heard he was going to Durham to read History, but now he was here in the stamp dealer's shop, stocky and florid, shedding Brylcreemed dandruff on the glass counter, a martyr to Stanley Gibbons, while his widowed mother hovered in the doorway to the living quarters. Smallbone, Andrews remembered, had a bitter loathing of stamps and the stamp trade.

'We're just closing,' said Mrs Smallbone, squinting through her ornate antlered spectacles.

'It's all right. It's a friend,' said Smallbone.

'Tea's ready, Derek.'

'In a minute.'

'Make sure you lock up.'

Smallbone stood very still for a moment or two without breathing. Then he relaxed.

'Let's go in the park,' he said. 'I need a smoke.'

They crossed the road into shady greenness and walked beside the pond.

'I heard you're at Blake's,' Smallbone said, lowering himself glumly on to a bench and accepting a cigarette. 'Mrs Abbott does the church flowers with my Mum. They know the secrets of all hearts.'

'I bloody hope not. Anyway, it's only for a term.'

'Seen Bruckner?'

'Seen is not the word. Endured Bruckner. Suffered Bruckner. I can't stay here, Derek.'

'Then don't. Get a bus to the station and fuck off out of it.'

'You could do the same.'

'Oh, no, I'll be here when I'm fifty. Supposing they haven't stuck me in the nuthouse. But I'm going to the university to do a doctorate part-time. In a year or two. When my mother gets over Dad's death.' Smallbone trod out the cigarette stub and lit another from his own packet.

A group of Dame Clare's girls in boaters came past on bicycles. Andrews and Smallbone stopped talking, the better to look at the girls' bare legs. The girls pointedly ignored them and rode off laughing, out of the park.

'D'you ever hear of Deirdre Scanlon nowadays?' Andrews asked.

'My mother knew her mother. Deirdre was going to train as a librarian.'

'I remember.'

'But she didn't, for some reason. Why do you ask?'

'Nostalgia.'

'They used to say she was dead mucky.'

'They were right.' Andrews remembered that once she'd

bitten his lip until it bled.

'I've heard she works in the Dock quite often.' Smallbone sounded wistful now. Not out much of an evening. He took the packet of cigarettes out of his jacket pocket, then replaced it and patted the pocket with large, slow gestures.

'D'you fancy a pint after?' asked Andrews. 'I mean, it's Friday.'

'I'd have to see. It's, you know.' He nodded back towards the shop. 'She gets in a state. I mean, she's always in a state but it gets worse if I go out.'

'Thanks for the tip about Deirdre, anyway.'

'Give her one for me,' said Smallbone, fiercely, then turned and hurried off, pausing at the side of the road to look both ways.

★

Deirdre worked at the Dock, eh? The Dock had been a good place to get your head kicked in when the trawlers were back and the deckhands flooded the streets in their electric blue suits looking for trouble. It was a three-roomed boozer crammed into an end terrace next to the Jewish graveyard and the chocolate factory, beyond which lay the increasingly unemployed river. He probably wouldn't bother seeing if she was there.

It was early. Andrews took a longish walk, a slow preliminary crawl. They'd been covering over the storm drains, leaving the brick bridge parapets strangely abandoned on long grassy patches marking the old drainbeds among the bombsites. He passed a solitary house-end occupied by an ancient painted advertisement for Crossleys' Haberdashers, the shop in town where Auntie Bella had spent her entire working life. He could hear a diesel clattering out through the warm grey evening towards the coast.

His parents' house was only the other side of the park. At the very least he should ring home, but he'd only get dragged in. He slowed at a phone box but went on, shaking his head. He couldn't stand the prospect of their uncritical understanding, or the invitation to pull up a chair and join the family round the open flooded grave. These conditions, this bit of teaching, were going to be merely temporary. It was far too soon to fail, to admit failure. He turned away from the image of himself entering the classroom to take the register on Monday. He could not, surely, simply be *claimed* like this, as though by a disease.

The little streets between the park and the river, named for ports in North Africa and the Middle East, seemed strangely empty. This had been no man's land, the route to the desirable pubs, girls, the odd bit of draw. He realised he was in danger of becoming emotional and took himself into the Baths for a steadying pint. The smell of smoke and body odour was instantly narcotic. He ordered a pint and joined the line of early drinkers leaning along the bar, grog-blossomed, marooned men in and beyond middle age, their fingers khaki with tobacco, the racing pages and pints of mild before them like evidence in mitigation. He finished the first pint quickly and had another.

That was better. Six-thirty. Like old times. Everything was still to play for – still light, still warm, the streets behind the streets remaining to be discovered by the serendipitous turning of a corner. Girls were getting dressed to sneak out past parents horrified at the shortness of their daughters' skirts and the thought of the smirking degenerates waiting for them in shop doorways and bus stops. It was anarchy. Everything was possible.

He left the pub and took a deliberate zigzag route among the low narrow terraces, confirming for himself their consoling smell of teas cooking and the faint sounds of television from the front rooms. After a while he allowed himself to reach the river, gagging as always at the sewer-stink of the tannery. He walked downstream, watching the brisk khaki tide overtaking him silently in its narrow steep-sided trench. Soon the little swing-bridge came in sight, joining east and west, its roof-lantern always faintly lit, the old goods track crossing it, then curving away among hawthorn scrub towards the old feed-mills and scrapyards and the blind ends of further terraces. The east was for the mad. The west had the football team and the brewery. He went across on the narrow pedestrian footpath beside the railway track. Afterwards there was only a demolished street for a while, crowded with grubby elderbushes that had sprung up through the old bombsites. Then houses appeared, boarded, their roofs beginning to go. It was still early, so he went over the crossroads into the Jubilation, vast and blackened, an old-style Victorian piss-palace. Only the huge bar seemed to be open.

A haggard barmaid served Andrews a pint and some crisps, then disappeared, leaving him alone with a burly, iron-haired, gaberdined drunk in his fifties who stood looking hungrily at the upright piano by the huge cast-iron fireplace. Andrews wondered if the man was thinking of using the piano to light a fire, but instead he leaned forward, raised the lid of the keyboard and began to play and sing. There were moments when it seemed as if a tune and some words would coincide, but then they went their separate ways once more. They were replaced by melancholy random vamping discords offset by an impassioned yet gargling vocal line whose élan was inversely related to its coherence. There was love in there somewhere, loss, and betrayal and spurned fidelity maintained under challenging conditions all other temptations notwithstanding, and it rapidly became intolerable, like being hit on the head with a soup spoon.

'Will you bloody stop that, Bernard?' said the barmaid, coming back from the interior. 'Or I shall have to put you out.'

Bernard desisted instantly.

'All the waters of Arabia could not extinguish me,' said Bernard, quietly, and he lumbered away through the door of the Gents.

'*He* was a teacher,' remarked the barmaid with an inflexion which Andrews found a bit sinister. Could it be so obvious what he, Andrews, was in danger of becoming, or did the woman share the omniscience of Mrs Abbott and Smallbone's mother? He finished his drink and left.

The river curved back across the tussocky asphalt to meet him, then veered away again. He climbed the stone steps up to a second railway bridge. Cloud-streets approached from westwards, and he caught a late glint from the estuary, though the water could not really be seen from here. Darkness had been released into the air like ink into a glass, a thickening in the light barely noticeable as yet.

He crossed the road and looked down into the old dock: half a football pitch of dove-grey water, too small and silted and remote nowadays, and known for the pub that stood at its far end. *This is what you have lost,* he found himself saying. But it was not as if he had wanted to come back, was it? Not that he had returned and been denied entry to the lost world of Fridays and Saturdays. The words FERODO BRAKE LININGS were still there to be seen on the cast iron panels of the bridge parapet if he cared to look back.

This excursion was a bad idea. He could still go back to his digs and call it a night. He could read and get some sleep. But he went in by the side entrance, taking in a blast of bleach from the Gents, and pushing at the next door found himself in the bar. It seemed unaltered – the semi-circular bays with the red leatherette cushions, the opaque windows onto the street, the glass dome, the red lino, and the wooden bar-top gleaming after its opening-time polish. And there was Deirdre Scanlan, sitting behind the counter, smoking a cigarette and examining her nails.

She looked up but gave no sign of recognition. He ordered a pint, paid, then watched as she took change from the till. Her skirt was still short but she'd put on a bit of weight, and something strange had happened to her hair. She'd chopped it very short and henna'd it. The effect was aubergine, like a psychedelic skinhead girl gone wrong.

She handed him the change without looking at him.

'D'you not recognise me?' he asked.

Deirdre squinted at him as if he was a long way off.
'Sorry?'

'Mick Andrews. I was the Third Murderer in *Macbeth*.'
She nodded.

'Right. OK.' Her face remained expressionless.

And, Andrews forebore to say, *you fucked my brains out repeatedly over a period of three months in autumn 1970. So how was it for you?*

He drank half his pint in one disappointed gasp and made to move away.

'How's your mole?' she asked.

'I beg your pardon?'

'You had a mole on your back. It got nicked when we were youkno that time, at me Mum's.' Now she smiled, that naughty smile that promised sweaty fun in dangerous settings.

'Well, I'm still here,' he said.

'Need to get it seen to.' *Need to get* me *seen to. Need to give you a seeing to.* 'So what brings you here?'

'Out for a pint.'

'On your own?'

'It's early yet.'

'Are you staying at your parents'?'

'No. How are yours?'

'The fookin shop burnt down.'

'My God.'

'That's why I'm barmaiding here.'

'Was anyone hurt?'

'We couldn't get the snakes out. That was the worst part. Me Mum's in Woodley Hall now. Off her fookin head, poor cow. Me dad's no cop. He's got some fancy piece in Bridlington. They run a shop selling trophies.' She shrugged, as if exhausted by the inevitability of these facts. 'Gizza tab then.'

You were a grammar school girl, Andrews thought.

'I'm sorry,' he said. 'Give her my best wishes.'

'She wouldn't understand.' Deirdre seemed angry rather than distressed at the situation. She shrugged and took a Benson from his opened packet. 'So how long are you here for?'

'Not long.'

'Man of mystery, eh?'

'Full of surprises, me.'

'I remember. College boy and all.'

'I've finished now.'

'I never went. I was going to be a librarian.'

'Does it bother you?'

'I dunno. I mean, nothing's settled. Nothing's properly happened yet. Except the fire, I suppose.' She crossed her legs. Andrews wanted to fuck her there and then. She caught his eye. 'What's it like to be a success? Back from college. I bet there are lasses queuing up.'

'Can you tell me where they're doing it? Life's been quiet.'

'Right. You want another?'

He nodded and glanced round. The fruit machine maintained its phantom activity.

'Speaking of quiet.'

'It's dead these days. Supposed to be closing down.'

'Everyone used to come here.'

'I know. It was good. All you lot, all us girls from Dame Clare's. Yeah.' She smoked in silence for a while. He enjoyed looking at her. 'I can't remember why we split up,' she said. 'There was *Macbeth*, but then – Long time ago, eh?'

Three and a half years. You were fucking one of the roadies in the carpark at the school dance when I came outside to look for you.

'Only about a thousand years. Get me pension next week.'

'What you doing after?' she asked.

'No particular plans. A few pints.'

'Cause we can go to Nigeria. If you want.'

'I'm not with you.'

'Club Nigeria. How long have you been away?'

'Years. Where is it?'

'Only round the corner.'

Two beehived women of forty, dressed up like teenagers, came in screeching with ferocious laughter. Immediately they monopolised Deirdre's attention. They kept playing Andy Williams on the juke box: *Can't take my eyes off of you.*

Andrews took a seat beside the fruit machine and read the evening paper. A tramp had died when the derelict house in Gladstone Street where he was sheltering burnt down. Kids probably. Verdict: misadventure. That couldn't be right. Or was he supposed to have got what he deserved? If you were derelict you needed burning. A woman had fallen in the river. A fallen woman, it was greyly implied. It drove him mad the way the local paper hyphenated street-names as if it were still the eighteenth century and Richard Savage was found in Blowjob-Street after dining in Hardon-Lane. But that was London and this wasn't. It was a bad idea, being here. Retrograde. But what had he been expecting?

Deirdre, he could tell, was discussing him with the women. They looked over appraisingly. What am I, a piece of meat? he felt like shouting. He didn't mind, really. But evidently he couldn't hold their interest, since they went quickly back to nattering. He turned again to the paper, moved on to sport, prices on the fish dock, then the £5 bargain sales – tricycles, dolls' houses, child's football kit (worn once). This must be what middle age was like, passing the time away, bored and terrified. Next time he looked up Deirdre had come over with a tray and was placing a fresh pint and a copy of *Dalton's Weekly* in front of him, making sure he could see her cleavage.

'All right?' she asked, raising her eyebrows and looking

back in mock-exasperation at the two women by the bar.

'Lovely, yes.'

'Not long now.'

He raised his pint in salute. He had to admit he was pissed. Let the cards fall where they may. When Deirdre called time and dimmed the bar lights he went to the Gents and stood in the ammoniac waterfall roar looking out of the little window at the dark. He ought be getting home – not home, back to Mrs Whatsit's. He would just tell Deirdre and get going.

'You're not coming, are you?' she said with a sad little smile, when he met her in the doorway. She had put some lipstick on, and long dark earrings. He remembered her fierce prettiness and looked for it in her tired, affectionate face. The landlady appeared in curlers and slippers, wanting to lock up.

'Go on, then,' he said. 'If it's not far.'

'I told you.'

She took his arm in the dark street and led him away. Somehow they were closer to the city centre than he'd thought. These were the old three-storey houses built by the Victorian middle class and abandoned after the war for the remoter suburbs. It was a borderline district of cheap lets, dentists, the odd law firm. Club Nigeria occupied a basement. They went down the area steps and through a lit doorway. Seated at a sideboard in the maroon-painted hall, a girl with mascara like a raccoon silently took their money, watched over by an impassive black man in dark glasses.

'All right, Kofi? This is my friend Mick. He's a guest, OK?' Deirdre told him. Kofi inclined his head without changing his expression and gestured to indicate a further door. Inside, Donna Summer was playing through big speakers in a long dim space with silver foil walls and a number of old leather settees. There was a small dancefloor where two girls listlessly circled their handbags, waiting for the action to begin. Deirdre led him to the bar, where a bald, muscular man of forty-odd in a tight white t-shirt was reading a book. To one side of the bar lots of polaroids were pinned up – red-eyed celebrants on epic nights at the Nigeria.

'Deirdre, my lover! The usual to start with this evening? And you've brought a lovely friend. He's a quiet one, I can tell. Bottle of lager for him?'

Deirdre nodded.

'I want a proper drink. A Moscow Mule. This is Mick. He's shy but dynamic like.'

'Room for all sorts here, my lover. Take it from Uncle Lex. Busy tonight round the corner?'

'Dead.'

'There's not the money since the fish and that. It's nowt but a village really. All starve together.'

They went and sat on a settee, watching the two languid girls. 'Jungle Boogie' almost got Andrews on his feet but the effort was beyond him. Deirdre finished her drink and went back to the bar.

'Here, this'll sort you out,' she said, crouching in front of him. He leaned forward and she snapped a popper under his nose. He thought he was going to have a heart attack.

'Fucking hell, Deirdre.'

'Good though, innit. I'm having a dance, all right?'

He rose dizzily and went to the bar. While Lex was making Deirdre another Moscow Mule, he peered at the photographs. No one he knew. Then he looked back: in a Hawaiian shirt, sitting grinning shyly between two laughing young men, beside the panel of photographs, was Mr Thorne. He was raising a glass with fruit and an umbrella in it.

'D'you know this bloke, Lex?'

'Why?' said the barman, suddenly careful.

'I thought I recognised him.'

'Are you really here for the hunting, lover?'

'No, I mean, I didn't know him from here.'

Lex looked at him.

164

'I can tell you're from round here. You've been away though.'

'Quite some time, yes.'

'That's Maurice in the photograph. He used to come in now and again.'

'So, was he –'

'One of us? I would have thought so, Mick. I mean, look at the picture. That's Ronnie and little Les with him, by the way. Does it matter?'

'No.'

'Then why ask?'

'He used to teach at my school.'

'One of the posh lads, eh? Thought so. I was Stepney High, me, with all the rough boys.'

'I never knew.'

'Why would you? He needed to be very discreet.'

'He managed that, then.'

'He tried, poor love. But somebody found out. Couldn't just leave him alone to live his life. He never harmed anyone,' Lex was almost shouting now. He looked down, then placed the two drinks on the bar.

'So has he left?'

'Oh, aye, he's gone all right.'

Andrews knew his line of questioning was moronic, but it seemed too late to stop.

'Another school? Another town?'

'No.'

'But he doesn't come in any more.'

'He doesn't go anywhere, you dozy cunt. He's fookin dead. They dragged him out Albert Dock back in May.'

'I'm sorry.'

'Are you really? Excellent.'

'Don't get on to me, Lex. I'm only asking. He was all right.'

'Idle curiosity doesn't help, though.'

'It's not idle.'

'What are you going to do? Avenge him?'

'Eh?'

'See what I mean?' Lex shook his head dismissively.

'I'm the one who's got his job.'

'You what? Never!' Now Lex was nonplussed. His eyes widened. He snorted. 'You're a teacher? You don't want to be coming in here then, do you?'

'I'm not a teacher, really.'

'What are you then, really?'

'This is temporary. I dunno.'

'Not one of us, anyroad.'

'Just here with Deirdre.'

Lex sniffed and began to polish some wine glasses.

'Everybody reckons someone at the school was on to him.'

'They could have asked him to leave.'

'I don't think – I mean, obviously I can't *know* – that was enough for whoever. It wasn't the scandal part, or it wasn't only that. It was real, like - hatred, malice. He was a nice bloke, was Maurice, shy and nervous, but he had his friends here. And there was someone who couldn't let him alone. Fucking straights, they're all the fucking same. Begging your pardon.' Lex put down the dishcloth. 'The inquest said the balance of Maurice's mind was disturbed. The school said maybe overwork. Held in great esteem. Sadly missed. All that shit.'

'What's up? Where's me drink?' said Deirdre, joining them.

'D'you mind if we go?' asked Andrews.

★

'You don't have to carry on, you know,' said Deirdre. 'It's not all about endurance.'

'Eh?'

'You're not a bad fuck, but your mind's not on the job,'

she said, turning aside and reaching for a cigarette. 'Not to worry, though. I mean, I got there a while back.'

'You know what?' He laughed. 'You're really coarse.'

'And that's why you like to give us one. Cos I'm a mucky woman. Posh boy.' She turned and kissed him.

'You're too rich for my thin privileged blood, Deirdre.'

'Maybe you should go. I mean, you don't have to. Only if you want. Things on your mind, I understand.' She sat up and began to roll a joint. It was seven a.m, the skylight pale blue.

'Isn't it a bit early for that?'

'Nothing else to do.'

'You're meant to be a librarian. You could read a book.'

'I think you're a born teacher. Always knowing what other people should do.'

So this was Saturday. Next was unbearable Sunday. Then school. The fear never quite went away.

He imagined Thorne sinking through the waters of the dock, claimed by the mud and shit and prams and sofas on the black bed, then released, bloated, back to the upper air. It was beyond belief that this could have happened, here of all places, where people just tried to mind their own business and get on with dying, with or without the assistance of alcohol.

'I've got some smack,' Deirdre said. 'I've been saving it.'

'Something for the weekend.'

'What d'you reckon?'

'It's daft. You'll just fuck yourself up.'

'I'm not forcing you. I just wanted someone to try it with.'

'I can't be doing smack. I mean, look at me.'

'I only mean smoking it. No needles.'

'I'm a teacher.'

'So you admit it.' She took the burning end of the joint in her mouth and blew smoke into his lungs. His head reeled. 'Never mind. Another time.'

'I wish I had amnesia,' he said. 'Then I could start again.'

'The Social wouldn't let you.'

'Or I could change my identity.'

'Not round here, you couldn't. But you say you won't be stopping anyway.'

'What about you?'

She was rolling another joint.

'Born here, died here.'

'Don't be daft.'

'I'm just realistic. Someone like me never goes anywhere.'

'You don't know that. Times have changed.'

She inhaled and coughed.

'A gypsy woman told me. So there. Anyway, what's it got to do with you? – Eh, are you gonna propose?' She choked on her laughter.

★

He had only to look at Bruckner to see that he was responsible for Thorne's death. It had always seemed natural to assume that Bruckner's malice was fundamentally rhetorical and that therefore its verbal expression served as its own reward, simply confirming the master in his radically adversarial position. Bruckner believed he was a rebel against the fools he despised and controlled, the sons of solicitors and trawler skippers and doctors and fruit merchants, the best the city could come up with and in his view almost entirely without merit. If Bruckner had his way half the Oxbridge entrants would be stopped at the city boundary and sent clerking in the council offices until death. Bruckner was, essentially, a right cunt in possession of significant powers.

Sitting with his new sixth-form charges in their funeral suits, looking down from the balcony across the cowed Lower School on the benches below, Andrews watched Bruckner kick off the new school year in the continuing absence of the Head, leading this band of brotherfuckers through a rousing if dissonant rendering of *Lord, receive us with thy blessing, / Once again assembled here.'*

Someone could be taken out and shot at any minute. It was as if no one could leave, except in a box. This was the brutal hangover talking, but let it have its say. It said the school was a recycling plant for dead people, like a miniature form of Buddhism with corporal punishment on top. They were all fucked from the outset and fucked at every stage thereafter until they died and recommenced being fucked. Andrews realized that he could hardly distinguish himself from the boys who sat in the rows around him. They might well be former masters themselves, having to re-sit their entire lives yet again. It was beyond him to act. He felt sick and slid out of his place to rush to the Masters' lavatory, where he retched with loathing and wiped his face with a paper towel the colour of shit and the texture of sandpaper. *This is temporary*, he told himself in the mirror. *This is temporary.*

He took the register. There were eight in the group, waiting watchfully, careful not to sit at the front. He gave out copies of the anthology.

'Sir, are you instead of Mr Thorne?'

'Because he died, sir.'

'So I understand. And it was very sad. I suppose, yes, I am, actually, if not grammatically, "instead of Mr Thorne". Now if you turn to page eighty, we'll begin reading Larkin's "Mr Bleaney".' Andrews listened to himself with remote disbelief. He could do this, God help him. 'If you have any questions – sensible ones – then don't hesitate to ask.'

Andrews had had the poem by heart for years. As he read the first verse, the close of the poem was already repeating itself in his head:

'But if he stood and watched the frigid wind

Tousling the clouds, and lay on the fusty bed
Telling himself that this was home, and grinned,
And shivered, without shaking off the dread

That how we live measures our own nature,
And at his age having no more to show
Than one hired box should make him pretty sure
He warranted no better, I don't know.'

When he finished reading the poem he told the class to read
it themselves in silence and get an initial acquaintance with
it. Then they would talk. After a while a hand went up,
Andrews nodded.

'Sir, he's lying, isn't he? The poet, I mean. He *does* know.
It's obvious.'

'Anyone care to take up that point?' asked Andrews,
glancing out across the rugby pitch. Far off, beyond the
railway, fairground vehicles had already begun to arrive. Soon
it would be October. After that, Guy Fawkes. Christmas. He
would ring his mother this evening.

Behind the Rain

for Alistair Elliot

So altered since last year his pen is –
I think he's lost his wits at Venice –
Byron, 'Epistle from Mr Murray to Dr Polidori'

Randall decided to stay on after the conference. He could afford it, more or less. Stay there, live simply. Get some work done on the book. Another two or three weeks, even a month, would be no problem, supposing he could arrange accommodation somewhere. He was on leave, and now there was nothing to compel him to go back to Durham before the New Year. All that other business was over. The only problem was that many places closed when autumn came. Venice for the Venetians: acqua alta and depopulation. To Randall the idea of such dank solitude was nearly erotic.

As luck would have it, Professor Fratini and his wife were about to leave to spend the autumn in Germany. When Randall mentioned his hopes of remaining, the Professor immediately invited him to make himself at home in the family apartment. The generosity was startling yet typical. It would be a point of honour to have Randall stay; the leonine Professor would be incurably insulted if he did not. By the evening, the elegant silver-haired Signora Fratini was showing him round, switching on the lamps as they made their way through the vast, dim chambers, explaining that while normally their daughter would mind the apartment in their absence, she too was away this year. The couple's luggage waited in the hallway.

Randall immediately knew where he would work – in the spare room. It held a bed, a desk, an old wash-stand and a tall mirror; it overlooked a back canal, with a glimpse of the roof of the Stucky Mill across on Giudecca far to the left. Opposite – perhaps only a dozen feet away – there rose a vast high wall of ashy stone, where the narrow, arched windows had all but one been bricked up. No light showed in the remaining window. There was no footpath on that side of the canal. It was perfect, a place to focus.

The three of them lingered over supper. 'There are far nicer rooms than the one you have chosen,' said the Signora, amused yet slightly disappointed. 'You could have a view.'

'I know. The apartment is wonderful. But I need to concentrate.'

'But you are constructing a cell. You are not a monk!'

'Not quite.'

'Will you not be lonely, Dottore?'

'I hope not. Or if I am, I hope it will be worth it. I have plenty to get on with.'

'You think you will finish your book here?' asked the Professor, with a knowing smile. 'It is easy to be distracted in Venice.'

'I hope I shall manage.' Randall did not add that it was now or never. It was all – all the bits and shreds and notes on notes – on his laptop. After all the mess and misery, if the collection was ever going to be finished – well, this was the best chance he was likely to get. No distractions. Besides, he must repay the Fratinis' generosity by showing it to have been wisely invested.

'Surely there must be young lady somewhere in the picture?' the Signora asked. 'She too would of course be welcome to join you.'

'Why not?' said the Professor. 'Let her enjoy it too.'

'I'm afraid there is no such person,' Randall said. 'The position is currently vacant.' There was a pause, while the Signora waited for him to explain.

'That is very sad,' she eventually added. 'But Franco, we could of course make some introductions –'

At the same time as Randall raised his hand in horror, which he hoped looked like self-deprecation, the Professor broke in with his satyr's chuckle.

'Giovanna, leave our young poet alone! If he wants to mortify his flesh we must let him discover how well he likes it. And I am sure he can find female company for himself if he feels the need of it.' The Signora shook her head and smiled. There was no helping in this case, clearly.

The couple bickered happily for the rest of the evening, until at midnight Randall excused himself and went away with a set of keys, promising the Signora that he would at least allow himself some recreation now and then.

In the morning, as he packed up his things in the almost-empty pensione in Cannaregio, he thought: now, for a little while, I shall live like a Venetian. To prove it, he followed some departing backpackers to the railway station and waved them anonymously off. Then he walked back along the Grand Canal until he could take a traghetto across to San Polo, relishing the coppery glitter and slide of the water. It was a fair distance to carry luggage to the Fratinis, and there were easier ways than walking, but now that he was alone he wanted the streets, the sudden emptiness, the next thing that lay down the next alleyway or over the sudden hump-backed bridge, the potential more important than the substance. In this, he thought, lay self-possession, in the unburdened curiosity of the traveller at rest, with memory in its right place, far away, long ago. He would be 'untalkative, out of reach', as the poet put it. Not that he would be pursued in any case. All that was definitely over.

He paused as he let himself into the apartment, his heart sinking slightly at the absolute quiet. It was like sadness and regret, like the ghost of grief, but it was not the same, not real. How could it be? He had come away from all that. He sneaked out again to buy bread and milk, then made a second attempt to take up residence. Without the exuberant Professor and the tall, poised Signora, the apartment was just so *big*, touched by that faint polish-smelling coolness of a place that was in it for the long run. The gaze of such an apartment would pass over the likes of Randall and scarcely bother to take him in. He could never be the subject of this place. But that didn't matter, did it? In fact, it was the whole point, to be anonymous here, not to matter.

To work. He set up the laptop and the little printer on a table at the window, laid out his notebooks, fetched a lamp from the library and wheeled in a comfortable high-backed captain's chair from the Professor's study. He made coffee. Then he sat gazing grimly into the screen at the wreckage of the manuscript. The poems lay there looking irredeemable. He could say the work was in transition, but to what? Yet however bad it seemed, the thing was to begin. He was not a novice.

Nor was he lazy, but he had been struggling to a degree unprecedented in his experience, reaching the point where the very idea of writing had begun to make him anxious. He always expected to worry and sweat, to be frustrated, to take out his frustrations by going on the lash now and then. All that was within the normal scale. He did not expect to be afraid, however – and that word that most nearly described the clenched, parched sensation with which he had been waking for the last few months, dragged rawly into consciousness at exactly half past three in the morning. The holiday mood of the conference, the company of poets and readers, had simply thrown a light disguise over the real state of affairs. He had hoped to sneak up on himself, to put failure behind him, to forget the pleas and phone calls and feeble shame. Now there was only himself, the page, the screen and the spartan room and the high wall opposite, with its one dark window.

Before, in what he now thought of as a lost world, he had been confident enough to follow the prompting of a poem as it began to emerge in a phrase or the shape of a rhythm. He had been patient, attentive, and, he now realised, lucky. Those days were gone. Now, it seemed, he must initiate the process by an effort of longing and persistence. So now he began by doing the three hours' work he had set himself as a daily target. Lines and phrases formed up one after another because he demanded that they do so, but like a bored mistress the language withheld its true favours, offering instead only limited, spiritless compliance. He re-read the pages and felt like taking a vaporetto to the airport immediately. Go back and teach. Forget about writing. Ordinary life cannot be as bad as this. The past is over. Make a living and be quiet.

But if nothing else, he had told the Fratinis he would stay. They were pleased to have someone keeping an eye on the place. He shut the laptop, put on his raincoat and went out for some air. It was a mellow evening at the edge of autumn, with the sun pausing for a moment to place gold-edged detail on the moving lip of shadow in the water beneath a bridge, all the while slowly claiming back its heat from the stucco and marble.

This was all Randall wanted really, he thought – to wander here with nothing in mind and nothing to say about it, to be as it were amid the interior of the art-world. All the books had already been written, the Aspern papers burnt, Aschenbach's fate settled, Beppo returned to Laura from the sea and Casanova escaped across the leads. The evening air, with its thread of cold and damp, like the effect of a banner flapping far off out to sea, felt like his element. He sought out remote bars to drink coffee and *grappa*. Without listening, he heard the conversation of the locals, who did him the courtesy of ignoring the preoccupied stranger who sat in his raincoat at a draughty table on the edge of their piazza.

As part of his discipline, he slept on the bed in his study, though there were plenty of more comfortable berths in the apartment. This must once have been a servant's room, though the Fratinis did energetically for themselves. The first night he found he could not read, so he lay imagining those centuries of confined, invisible, uncomplaining, mostly female lives, chained to a class he supposed largely vanished now. He drowsed with these thoughts, then woke for a moment, wondering what that sound could be. He realised it was rain, plunging down the narrow gap between the houses and into the empty canal. He was surprised to find next morning that otherwise his sleep had been undisturbed. It was, he remembered thinking, like the pause between movements in music, temporary but welcome nonetheless. It was a form of afterwards, the preface to a new life.

By day, though, the dry spell persisted. The page was like a desert, with neither features nor relief from the glare of its tedium. Only discipline could save him. Though he longed to be outside, walking, feeling the early cold on his face, he kept his promise to the desk, did what he must and what he could. His release at noon felt like a pardon following false imprisonment – with himself as the gaoler too. *Cui bono?* he wondered.

As far as possible on his noonday walks he avoided the major sites – the Rialto, San Marco, the Accademia - preferring the closed views of the remoter squares and canals. He liked the roofed alleyways, and the dark, damp little yards crowded with windows and doors, so tall that the dove-grey sky itself seemed like a visitor or a rumour. He was taken with the idea that the city was larger than it looked, its additional streets standing up when required like scenery, otherwise packed neatly away on the inside of their own shadows. The gusty autumn weather, with its unpredictable bursts of rain and shafts of low sunlight, seemed apt to this, as though the world had been driven half indoors. *Write it down*, he thought, and grimaced.

More than once he was turned back by flooded alleyways; more than once he failed to find his way back to a little piazza with a secret bar in which he had been the only customer. There was, he now felt, something indefinably erotic about this slow, random exploration. All this was at least the cousin of happiness – enough to give him the strength to go back and revise the morning's work in late afternoon before slipping out again towards dusk to resume his wanderings.

It was a week before he saw her. It happened as he approached the apartment at seven pm – he had stayed out far longer than usual, and was feeling guilty at this neglect of his desk. She was crossing a narrow bridge near the apartment – a dark-haired girl in a white raincoat. He would hardly have looked, except that she stopped at the top of the bridge, then raised a bunch of dark roses she was carrying and sank her face among the blooms. The private gesture, in a half-public place, with, it seemed, Randall the sole observer, was oddly stirring, as though he had been invited to trespass. He paused, approaching the bridge, then felt self-conscious and pressed on to pass the girl, who looked up without interest as he went by. When he allowed himself to look back, she was gone.

Psychologists and the police like to claim that we see more than we know. The witness takes in a mass of detail: it is simply a matter of finding access. The girl's face clarified itself unbidden in Randall's mind as he went up the stairs to the apartment – lustrous skin touched with gold, dark eyebrows that could be stern, green eyes, a wide, negligent, impatient mouth lipsticked in deepest red, as though to match the roses in her hands. A beauty, obviously, but hardly unique in Italy, in Venice, or here in Dorsoduro. He had not realised how closely he had looked. Was he coming back to life? He was smiling as he opened the door: she, on the other hand, had taken no notice of him whatever. The homage of the gaze had all been going in the right direction. No danger there: his presence was not required, never mind desired, and therefore could not be rejected.

The repairs to be made to that morning's work seemed a smaller matter than usual, though they cost him the same dislike and the trapped, dangerous anger unique to someone whose very language has turned against him. Once more the idea floated itself that if he simply stopped work it would not be the end of the world; but that of course was exactly what it would be, since he as he understood himself, Randall the Writer, the poet, servant of a vocation, would cease to exist, and then what would become of him? Anyway, he did the work. He got through it, whatever that meant. Then he opened a bottle of the Fratinis' cold white wine and sat idling at his desk, knowing he should get something to eat.

The wall opposite was in full shade, the outline of the window faintly visible. After a while he turned away, glancing idly at the tall mirror propped by the foot of the bed. Then something moved there in its liquid depths, a flash of white that seemed to half-turn as it crossed the mirrored space and just as quickly vanished. Automatically Randall looked out into the dimming air, at the window opposite, for the source of the reflection. Nothing. Or was there a faint glimmer some way back from the window itself?

It was already too dark to say with certainty. It might have been a lone gull cruising the canal, though he did not remember seeing such a thing before now. It was something or nothing, an effect of light, and, after all, not important – except to someone like him, tired now and bored with himself. He re-corked the half-empty bottle, returned it to the refrigerator and went to bed, once again finding himself unable to read.

When he woke, having slept nearly ten hours, he knew he was emerging from a crowded dream-event, but nothing, not an image, not a word or a flicker, had come back to the waking world with him. He had sweated heavily during the night. He showered, dressed and resumed work, grinding out his pages until he heard noon strike outside.

His footsteps led him back to the little bridge around the corner. It was colder and windless today. The tied-up boats looked as though embedded in the green immobile water. He stood aside as an old couple came past, silently companionable with their bags of groceries, paying him no mind, as if all the strangers were really gone from the city by now. He stood irresolutely for a minute or two, then struck off southward, deciding to give himself a good hour for a walk. The dream went with him, revealing nothing of itself but resting on his thoughts as though against a concealed door.

As a result he saw nothing of his surroundings until he arrived at San Nicolo dei Mendicoli. Here it was truly cold. The church took the brunt of the chill wind blowing in off the lagoon along the Zattere. It was undergoing restoration and completely enclosed by a corrugated iron fence. The effect was forbidding. The pleasure on which he had come to depend drained rapidly away. In irritation he turned aside to follow a stretch of canal he did not know.

After a hundred yards or so it turned left, and he saw that a stretch had been dammed and drained. In the bare trench, yellow and khaki mud gleamed with a vile fluorescence in the grey air. In the canal banks the rotted bricks and mortar and the ancient wooden revetments and pilings were glistening, grey and diseased. Pumps took up the slow leakage sweating from the wooden dams, but there was no one at work presently. Randall lingered, sickened and fascinated. He had known perfectly well that these side canals had no depth – ten feet at most – but it was necessary to think otherwise, to suppose them to contain fathom on enchanted fathom, reflections stacked inexhaustibly on each other. Otherwise – he could not think what.

Defeated, he made his way slowly back to the apartment, wondering if after all he would have to renege on his agreement. If he could not at least enjoy the city, what reason was there to remain?

As he turned the corner he saw the girl a little way ahead of him crossing the bridge. He was sure it was her – the same thick dark hair, the white coat. He accelerated a little without knowing why. She turned left, which would bring her along the outside of the Fratinis' building. The sound of her heels came back off the surrounding walls. When he turned the corner she was nowhere to be seen, but unless she had broken into a run this could not be so. And anyway, he could still hear her footsteps nearby, keeping the same brisk but unhurried pace. He ran the length of the building and looked down the narrow streets to either side. Nothing. Now the footsteps faded from earshot.

He smiled. Obviously he knew nothing about Venice. He was just a visitor, like all the rest; the fact that he had stayed on said nothing about him. A few rambles in its quiet parts had taught him very little. Anyway, it was good to think that the place was bigger where the Venetians were concerned. And you couldn't go round following girls just because you felt like it. There were manners. There were laws, even. He reached into his pocket for the key to the courtyard door. As he stopped he heard footsteps, heavier this time, a man's footsteps, approaching. He turned to look, but the sound was gone. Then as he turned to push the outer door closed again, it seemed he could hear the heavy tread going on its way, a little distant now. As he went upstairs to the apartment, he realised that he was a little aroused by the idea of the imaginary pursuit. *What wild ecstasy? What maidens loth?*

He completed his revisions without interest and then sat with a glass as dusk came along the little canal. He decided not to switch on the lamp. After a while he turned in the chair so that he could look into the mirror. It was larger than he had thought, the size, really, of a small door, with decorative black edging, something made locally, he imagined, on Murano, old, but he had no idea how old, and with a slightly tired look, as though in need of refreshment and a touch of silver nitrate. The mirror should have a gloomy signature tune of its own, a piano piece, never quite clear or fully resolved, as though heard in a stairwell from an unvisited room. Should he make a note of that? He refilled his glass and sat on.

He had to blink to confirm that the movement had recurred. There it was – the momentary whiteness turning, curling, sinking back into the darkened surface. He looked out at the window opposite: nothing moved. He looked back, and the movement recurred. He sat forward. Whatever appeared in the glass must be reflected from somewhere, obviously. It would be a question of angles, something from the realm of physics, but he'd quickly given up listening to that at school. No matter: what he wanted was a clearer view.

He blinked, then looked back. The movement came again, and this time it was a little clearer. A skirt. It was a skirt, a wide, white skirt, and someone was turning in it, swinging it as she did so, perhaps to relish the movement, to see how the garment would hang when it ceased to move. Now the figure came closer, the dark head turning aside as she fiddled with something, an earring perhaps. When the mirror suddenly emptied Randall realised he had been holding his breath. He stood up and looked out of the window. Nothing was visible opposite. Nothing moved. He sat down again.

Now the woman returned to the mirror, closer, leaning in to apply lipstick, with that neutral appraising gaze that had always excited him. He loved to watch his girlfriends making up. When for the first time he could see her face properly it was the girl from the bridge, the brow, the wide mouth boldly emphasised, the green gaze of unworried challenge. She went on looking as she put the top back on the lipstick, then stepped back out of sight with a final coquettish twirl of the skirt.

He felt light-headed with shock. You are a voyeur, he thought, as he stood in the kitchen drinking grappa. But could that technically be true, given that the source of what he witnessed was not directly available? Couldn't optics in some way diminish responsibility? Anyway, he hadn't seen anything improper, had he? More than that, the woman had clearly been looking into *her* mirror. But she couldn't see *him*, could she? Otherwise she'd have given some sign. Then again, she'd ignored him in the street, though of course she had no reason to notice him there. His head rang with these absurdities, expecting a sleepless night. It was eight a.m. when he woke, heavy with the backwash of another escaped dream.

During the day the rain set in properly. Randall re-read his work and closed the notebook, wrote nothing, and, for once, did not go out. To read a page of a novel was an unequal struggle. The evening was slow to come. The rain fell steadily. He waited in his chair, turning between the mirror and the window.

He must have dozed, for when he looked up the girl had returned to the mirror, moving behind the reflected raindrops, but seeming clarified or magnified rather than blurred. He sat forward. Tonight she held out a short red dress before her, giving it the same critical gaze as yesterday's, then drew the garment against herself, tilting her head to one side in slow consideration. Her eyes emptied momentarily as her attention seemed to wander out of the frame of the mirror, as if she were listening for something. Then, matter-of-factly, she slipped the dress over her arms and head, giving a glimpse of the silky whiteness of her underthings before she adjusted the skirt. Next, briskly, the lipstick. Once again the objectivity of her gaze excited Randall. Earrings. Perfume. Then she stood as though taking her own salute. Appeased, she reached for a small black handbag, then half-turned, nodding, before glancing momentarily back into the mirror. She smiled and stepped out of view.

She has company, thought Randall, going to the window, his heart banging in his chest. The window opposite maintained its discreet darkness on the other side of the rain. She was talking to someone.

What he felt was an inextricable mixture of jealousy and excitement. Things have changed, irrevocably, he thought, and then *What things?* What he had been seeing was clearly an accident, an anomaly, a trick of the light which only seemed uncanny because he couldn't account for it. But since he could barely change a bulb for himself, his doubts meant very little in this context. More important, none of this — whatever this might be — was any of his business. He was trespassing on the girl's privacy. He should stop. He must. At the same time, her presence seemed like a challenge, insistent: pay attention, look, look at me. But that could not be so either. *Either you stop this now or you have to make contact,* he thought, frightened and aroused.

Once more he slept heavily. He woke as though hungover, but had drunk no more than two glasses of wine. Outside, the rain persisted. The opposite window looked indifferently back.

In the shower he decided to take a complete break. Against his rules, he walked to the Rialto. The city waited in the rain, water lapping over the raised river-steps of the palazzi on the great curve of the canal. There was hardly anyone about. He made his way north to the Fondamente Nuove and joined a handful of older people waiting at the jetty for a boat out to the islands. This morning San Michele, the cemetery island, was barely visible across the water, merely an area of grey cross-hatching inside the grey wash of low cloud and water.

A burly double-decker *motonave* emerged through the gloom, and the passengers boarded to sit in silence and as far from each other as possible. Beyond Murano, where several people disembarked and no one got on, the waters widened into a blankness that Randall found restful. The posts marking the channels loomed, their lights blinking, topped by solitary white gulls, planted squarely like inspectors. Today this all seemed like an allegation of solidity in these rain-beaten lead and silver reaches where surely no such thing was to be found. Again, Randall approved. Let things fade and dissolve, and let consciousness go with them. Make a renunciation. Let what happened happen. He grew calmer.

After Burano only one other passenger remained aboard. When they docked at Torcello, Randall gestured to the old gentleman to go ahead of him. The stranger gravely raised his hat in acknowledgement and disappeared into the rain.

As he set out along the footpath beside a small canal, Randall wondered why he had bothered to come. It wasn't sights he was after – or not these sights, at any rate. But he went on, hunched in the rain, over the Devil's bridge, past the closed restaurants and their sopping gardens. Because he thought he should, he revisited the old basilica, taking in the details of Hell in the frescos and sensing a true wintry cold prefigured in the vast, faintly ringing chamber. Afterwards he wandered over the rain-silvered grass to the low wall that looked out over the reed-banks towards less-visited islands, none of which could now be seen. Though the damp was making him ache, he felt the strange contentment he remembered from sitting in the pavilion watching the rain cancel a match. Failure was impossible under such circumstances because the contest had not been undertaken. Nothing would be so important that the weather could not cancel it. They would take tea and have another look and nothing would happen, and when the rain slackened a little the master would tell them to load the kit and get back on the coach for home, and the Pocklington match would have to wait another year. It was all very satisfactory.

Randall had known at the time that it wasn't the cricket he was concerned with - just as, he thought, watching the rain thrash down on the reeds, somehow this business with the girl and the mirror was an effort by something inside him to get him to admit defeat, to acknowledge that some things were unattainable. There were no more poems to be had. The couple of collections he'd published would either survive or they wouldn't, and he would have to make do with that. Most people had to make do. It was no dishonour. You couldn't simply invent water in a desert, just as you couldn't invent love. Only God could do that. And how important, really how important, was it to him in the end? Hadn't he been protesting too much? Take pleasure in the mysteries of things, and let language look after itself. He turned his face upwards to the rain. It pelted against his skin and ran down beneath his collar. He let it fall into his mouth.

Randall knew as he approached the dock that the old man in the shelter would seek to engage him in conversation. He didn't much want to talk. He had spoken to almost no one for days, and felt that he would be breaking some kind of covenant if he did more than exchange courtesies. But so what? Let it be. Let his fellow traveller speak if he wished.

The old gentleman raised his hat once more and indicated that Randall might sit on the bench beside him. He had carefully oiled white hair with traces of the odd Venetian blondeness, a neat moustache and pale blue eyes.

'Have you enjoyed your outing, Signor?'

'I suppose so,' said Randall, with a smile. 'It's not the best day for it, maybe.'

The old man tilted his head to indicate that this was questionable.

'It is not all a matter of liking.'

'How so?'

The old man lit a Nazionale and seemed to have forgotten Randall's question.

'Why are you here, Signor, may I ask? The season is clearly over.' He gestured at the weather.

'To work,' said Randall.

'But you are not working, unless your work is to wait for a boat with an old man in the rain.'

Randall thought it would be too difficult to reply properly. But he also noted that he felt no resentment at the intrusion, the questioning of his purpose.

'I am stuck, Signor,' he replied, 'frustrated. I cannot go on with my work, it seems.'

'Your employer must be very generous.' The old man smiled, as though life were a maze of such burdens and evasions.

'I am my employer.'

'Then perhaps you should take a firmer line.'

They laughed.

'I have tried,' Randall said, 'but it seems I do not mend my ways.'

The old man nodded, breathing out smoke.

'Some things will keep a man from his work. In your case I think perhaps there is a woman?'

'I'm sorry?'

'You bear the marks, my friend. You have suffered in an affair of the heart.'

Randall stared at him.

'How would you know such a thing?'

'Then I am wrong,' said his companion. 'My apologies.' The old man rose, peering out across the murk of the lagoon.

'You are not entirely mistaken, Signor. It is complicated,' said Randall. 'I am here partly to recover, I suppose.'

Without looking round, the old man nodded and made a sound of assent. Randall found himself waiting. The *motonave* had stolen up, its prow emerging from the fog, its cabins bleary blocks of light.

'So what do you suggest?' he found himself prompting.

'I would not presume.'

The boat was at the dock, a crewman preparing to throw a rope. It seemed very important to extract something from the old man.

'Perhaps we can continue our conversation on the return journey,' Randall said. Now the old man turned.

'I am not going back,' he said. 'This is where I stay now.'

Randall felt an inexplicable degree of disappointment. It was like shame.

'Then I will say farewell.'

The old man looked at him with a wintry smile.

'Safe journey, Signor, until you arrive behind the rain.' He raised his hat, nodded graciously, and set off back along the path inland.

I like that, thought Randall: *behind the rain*.

He found himself exhausted when he returned to the apartment. He showered to relieve the aching cold, then went to bed and slept for twelve hours. Next day he stuck it out at the desk for the morning but wrote nothing. Instead, he watched the rain falling into the canal. Nothing stirred in the window opposite. The mirror simply registered the rain. At noon he put on his hat and coat and went out.

He could not have said why he'd never previously tried to find the front of the building opposite his window. It simply hadn't come up. His wanderings had always led him away from it. Today, to begin with, he approached via the little bridge where he'd first seen the girl. The rain was heavy enough to make him think twice, but he went on. No one else was out in this.

The drenched air was blue with a faint fog that rose in corners and entrances. Instead of going left and southward as usual, he made his way along an alley. He supposed the right-hand wall must belong to the building in question – which must then be immense, an entire block, perhaps some grim inward-looking palazzo. No entrance presented itself – though one tall gateway had been bricked up - and the narrowness of the passage prevented him gaining any clear impression of the place. The alley turned sharp left at the end. When he found himself led away he accepted the diversion as normal, only to find that the compensating right-hand option never presented itself.

Reaching another small bridge, he turned back the way he had been compelled to come, but was not surprised to discover that without meaning to he had somehow rejoined his usual route back to the original bridge, though this was much nearer than he supposed. He leaned against the parapet, looking along the canal. He could make out his window, and the pillars of the window opposite. The water was black, fleetingly pitted with dull silver as the rain fell with steady heaviness.

A church bell sounded nearby. He checked his watch. It was already evening, though it could not be. He had only been walking for twenty minutes, surely. He stared into the dark water, shaken. Go back to the apartment, write the Fratinis an apologetic note, and get yourself home. You are losing it. He made his way round to the front door.

Once more he hesitated with the key, listening, then gave way to impulse and walked on to the far corner of the building. Here an alleyway led down towards the canal but it was cut off by a wall apparently with no other function. He took the right turn offered, and found himself moving along a narrow colonnade. The flagstones here were inch-deep in water, and he wondered at the stupidity of the mission he seemed to have undertaken.

After a time the canal narrowed slightly. Then it took a left turn, only to dead-end at a high brick wall where a couple of half-submerged boats were moored, seemingly abandoned. There was no way to go on. He made to turn back. But at some time there had been a bridge at this point, marked by raised flagstones on either side. And on the far side, tucked into the shadows, was a low entrance through which Randall could dimly see a further alley leading away.

The water was six feet wide. He could take a run-up of sorts, half a dozen strides. He would do it, or he wouldn't. If he didn't take the jump, he decided, he would simply leave Venice.

He ran up, jumped, landed on the half-sunk flagstone, slithered and nearly fell back into the canal, but managed to hang on to the remnants of the parapet. He laughed in the gloom and set off down the next alley. This too followed a high wall. To his relief it broke left and he emerged into a little piazza. The lights of a bar fell through an open wooden doorway set in a large double gate. He peered inside. Across a wide dark courtyard there were steps leading up to a further lit doorway in a wide high-windowed frontage. But now his nerve failed him. He went into the bar and ordered a beer. The place was deserted.

'Please, what is that building?' he asked the barman, pointing back across the street.

'Manicomio.' The man, bald and thick-set, shrugged and returned to his newspaper.

'Scusi?'

'Manicomio.' The man stood upright and made agitated movements with his hands about his head, sticking out his tongue, making his eyes bulge. 'Yes?'

'A madhouse?'

The barman shrugged and nodded.

'Si.'

Randall drank his beer.

'Strange that it stands alone. And doesn't open on to a canal.'

'There was a canal before, where the courtyard is. There was an island – like all Venice is islands, the city itself. You do not know this?'

'I hadn't thought about it like that.'

'But is all gone now. All those people. Chiuso. All closed.'

'Where have they gone, the people?'

The barman looked at him patiently.

'There are many madhouses, signor. They are everywhere.' He nodded towards the rain still falling outside and at Randall's dripping coat. Randall paid and left.

As he crossed the piazza the lights in the doorway beyond the gate went off. There had been nothing inviting about it before. Now his resolution threatened to fail him again. There was nothing to find, in any case. Better go back.

He stepped through the low gate into the courtyard.

Despite the rain and darkness he could see now that the building was immense, tall and wide-balconied and many-windowed in the Venetian style. It had the stopped look of a place no longer in use. Perhaps the light in the doorway was for security, in which case perhaps the timer needed fixing or something. He was at the foot of the broad, blackly-gleaming steps. There was no need to go on. As he had wished, he had identified the place. He had seen it. He was free to go back now. Any further and he would be trespassing.

He went slowly upwards, expecting to be stopped by a concierge or a cry from the distant street, but then he stood at the glass-panelled double door, with his hand on the fingerplate applying gentle pressure, and next he was inside, letting the door swing quietly back and standing for a moment, shocked by the quiet following the rush of the rain in the darkness outside, and by how easy it was to come in.

Stairs curved upwards on either side, he supposed towards the *piano nobile*. The dark air felt smooth and desiccated, as though preserved. He took the left hand flight, feeling his way as he moved beyond the faint light thrown from the piazza, until he came back within reach of the long dim rectangles of light laid down through the windows and between the shadows of the pillars. The vast *piano nobile* seemed completely empty, like a ballroom on the flagship of a defunct cruise line. He would, he thought, have to go up one more flight to reach the right floor, so he followed the next set of stairs through their half-circle up into the dark. It felt as if there was nothing here at all, scarcely even the idea of a place. But he could hear his own footsteps, mechanically ascending the stone steps.

At the top of the stairs was a broad corridor with a series of doors on the left side. At this height, the lights of the piazza reached the upper halves of the doors as well as parts of the moulded ceiling. By Randall's estimate, this should be the floor opposite the Fratinis' apartment. It was not too late to turn back. He had not been discovered. Honour was satisfied.

A sudden gust threw rain like gravel against the windows. There were nine doors, and he guessed that the fifth might lead to the window opposite his workroom. There could be no harm in checking. He moved down the passageway, glimpsing the storm-battered city across the roofs. At the fifth door he paused, as if he might still turn back, then tried the handle.

The door opened on a small narrow room in which he could just make out a further door at the far end. This time a key remained in the lock. He turned the key and opened the door into what he felt rather than saw was a smaller space. Stepping inside, he let the door swing closed behind him. There was an audible click: he was reminded of the sound a successful poem was meant to make as it was completed.

Here there were competing smells of musk and harsh disinfectant. The window was faintly outlined. He would simply check and go. He barked his shin against an iron bed-frame. Beside it he found a standing full-length mirror covered in a blanket, angled to the window. Having come so far, he thought, he was bound to have chosen the wrong room. It was all guesswork. Any room might have a mirror, and there was no way to identify the windows opposite.

He looked out through the rain. The canal below was a dark strip with darkness pouring into it. The window opposite might be his – hard to tell. There was a faint lamp-glow from the right. Nothing else.

He turned away, and as he did so there was movement opposite. Not possible. He peered out. There it was again, but no clearer. He stepped back in frustration and his hand brushed against the frame of the mirror.

Once more he looked out into the rain. Then pulled the blanket from the mirror. He sat on the end of the stripped bed and waited, he could not have said how long, lulled by rain and dark as though by sleep.

In its own time, the mirror woke and shapes emerged,

moving within it, surfacing through the rain that teemed across its surface.

The woman lay on the sheets, her head thrown back, her dark hair and her arms spread wide. The head of the lover moved across her breasts, then lower, beyond sight, while she spoke or cried out in silence until she wrapped her fingers in his hair and drew him back towards her, turning to hold him in her arms, still speaking silently, exposing Randall's own face to himself for a moment, the eyes shut, the mouth open with desire. Now he saw. Now he knew. He was sure, beyond the need of checking, that by now the door of the room was locked. What would the Fratinis think?

In the Duchy

In The Duchy, hereafter known as *The Duchy*, the climate has assisted in the creation of an unusually extensive literature, as a result of which the public libraries remain open on Sundays, far into the rainy evening. People are hungry to learn. Anything will do. You may infer – though, given the morose character of the inhabitants, the proposition is not susceptible to proof – that this is a cause of quiet satisfaction among a people whose national costume is the raincoat and where even the womenfolk go about in Homburg hats.

At the steamy doors they disrobe for the getting of wisdom. Every library has a bar where the syrupy beers of the region are sold in chalice glasses by bar-librarians who struggle to tear their eyes from whatever they are reading. Everyone understands the difficulty. Everyone smiles and turns the page, sitting steaming damply on stools and captain's chairs, heads bowed religiously before the wilderness of incurious and unconsulted bar-mirrors.

You are not reading this evening? Very well. You may sit as long as you like at your table outside the café by the theatre watching rain fall into your glass as a great host of guild members processes by in their parti-coloured tunics, dragging the axes and silvery horns of their various defunct trades across the cobblestones behind them on their way to the station - for few of them actually live here; very few people at all actually live here, and most of them will be in the reading rooms and carrels for some time yet.

The station brasserie to which the celebrants are wearily

tending after their masses and parades contains a number of murals by Delvaux, in which little girls in white dresses stand in imperilled contrast to the gleaming iron threat of the locomotives. Go there and you might never go anywhere again, so peculiar and apologetic is the sense of danger given off by these works.

Beneath them the departing travellers sit indifferently with their beer and charcuterie, talking in the desultory way of those who wish they were already elsewhere and kicking off their buckled shoes on the way upstairs to sleep off their re-enactments, books open on their breasts while rain falls on mossy skylights. At the same time, however, you may suspect that if you cease to give these travellers your full imaginary attention they may simply slip away from brasserie and platform via secondary exit tunnels in a spontaneous unofficial strike on behalf of the extras of history. You are in two minds whether to continue to sustain them. If they think they are tired they should try being you.

Still, you can picture them perfectly from where you sit, as the lamps come on like stage-lighting around the smoke-furred roof-parapet of the Theatre Grand, as you look into your empty glass and consider what the evening holds for you, as your thoughts release the (perhaps) bogus pilgrims back into their unthinkably specific lives.

Best to order another beer – though beer is not the word - to feel its thick, sweetly baleful influence rise through your sinuses and brain-pan, like a slow interior drowning. Sit and peel a painted egg, then salt it and savour it slowly while the rain bounces off the metal table and surfs up round the wheels of the secretaries' heavy bicycles as they hurry from the language schools to get an hour in at the library. Strange that anyone should need to be taught *language*, since without it what could be accomplished anyway? Money for old rope, you suppose. And where do the learners come from? Surely everyone is here already.

Into the pause after you reach the far end of this beery

oxbow lake of enquiry a faint anxiety admits itself like a polite official in a suit, looking round a door, not wanting to be a nuisance but nonetheless needing to persist. It will be best not to enquire too closely into how you yourself came to be here in your sodden dog-smelling overcoat, eating the egg and drinking the beer. *Behind every fortune is a great crime* passes through your mind, but the precise role you occupy in relation to the statement is not provided. You don't mind especially which it is; but (without going so far as to commit yourself to the enquiry) you think it might be best to know – that is, if one could both know and not know, which ought to be possible, if it is the case, as Bacon and Montaigne attest, that in contradiction lies, in a nutshell, the primary manifestation of the human state. Villain, ingénu, asthmatic policeman, judge, landlady, schoolgirl, priest, assassin, gravedigger, actuary… Anything there take your fancy? No hurry. The evening stretches out in front of you like a lifetime, greying and dimming, slowly, second cousin to immortality.

Leaving a coin or two for the waiter, you rise and go over the cobbles and round the corner into the beginnings of dusk, the Duchy's finest drizzle slicking your hair and weighing down the heavy brown travelling coat (but what is a staying-at-home coat?) as efficiently as the pair of bricks an intending suicide might stuff in his pockets before leaving his apartment to step off the wall of the little stone bridge you are crossing now. Have a look over the edge for yourself: two swans rest in the shadow of the arch, their heads folded for sleep. You wonder if it's true what they say about swans. And surely the water is too shallow to drown in. From the nearby zoo, you hear the evening trumpeting of the elephants. When the first zoos were introduced to Europe, the public attacked the animals. Here and now, though, it's peaceful, sedative even.

For a moment you worry where to turn. This liberty is almost too much. You let the route suggest itself, between two confectioners' shops, up a curving alley of dark ochre brick with herringbone paviour. A radio is playing faintly in an upper room. The sense of expectation is unsettling: at some point this – call it by its name – this *flanerie* will have to produce a sense of arrival, of being here rather than elsewhere, here with an end in view. The rain is heavier and colder now.

You find you have paused in front of a shop window where bald naked mannequins, their white skin slightly lustrous and grubby like ping-pong balls, stare haughtily out into the evening. How, you wonder, would someone happen into the way of manufacturing such figures, and how are their faces and their expressions chosen? Are they, as Marianne symbolises France, symbolic of a particular branch of commerce – dressmaking, perhaps, its proud traditions, its victories and legends and self-sustaining love? Will the nation-state survive the commercial ingenuity even of such tiny specialised enterprises as this?

A wide white straw hat with a turned-up brim, such as Audrey Hepburn might have worn for a fashion shoot in the 1950s, descends on the head of the mannequin in front of you. You nod, approvingly – it sets off the figure's featureless nakedness quite well. Audrey would never have allowed herself to be photographed like this, of course.

Now out of the gloom a figure appears beside the mannequin – a small, fierce-looking, bespectacled middle aged woman in a dark suit. She is gesturing at you. You raise a hand politely. Her gestures grow more vehement. Her mouth opens silently. She is pointing up the street. She wishes you to follow her directions. Is there a problem? Are there robbers in the shop? Is there a fire? No, she wishes you to go away. She repeats the gesture, wearing a rictus of disbelieving anger. How dare you? Now you are ashamed, though you intended no offence. Your interest in the nude mannequins was purely philosophical – though now that she has drawn your attention to the matter it is possible to discern certain erotic overtones in the scene. Yet to the pure all is pure. You hurry off up the narrow street, averting your gaze from the dim windows of a succession of antiquarian bookshops.

At the end of the street there appears a small cinema, The Rex. The façade is lit. There are pictures of William Holden and Rita Hayworth in little cases. But there is no one at the ticket booth. On impulse you push through the doors into the darkness.

The auditorium smells of dust and sweat and chocolate. There seem to be few other people there for the evening showing. Several of them are reading by the light of pencil torches. Stepping over the legs and the pike of a snoring drunk in a uniform of the Napoleonic era, you go closer to the front and sit at the end of a row. You have missed part of the supporting programme – a short documentary about the fishing industry of the Lofoten Islands. It is subtitled but the narrator's voice seems to belong to Valentine Dyall, the Man in Black. He brings the same sense of sombre imminence to this subject as to the hauntings and curses and comeuppances for which he is famous throughout the English-speaking radiophonic world. You yourself cannot care so greatly for fish and fish products, nor for the Lofoten Islands, and you find yourself studying the cloud-streets of cigarette smoke as they advance through the beam of the projector. It is like a childhood illness, a state of listless suspension moving at the slow implacable pace of an adult truth.

At last the main feature begins. This too is subtitled – *Nazi Treasure of the Devil* – though the English title is *Operation Amsterdam*. A war movie from the 1950s, starring Peter Finch and Eva Bartok. You have seen it before but you surrender yourself to the monochrome of world conflict – smoke rising over the docks, sirens, gunfire, capacious mackintoshes, under-written female roles – yet it is not the performances or the plot that beguile you. It is the city itself – all those untaken streets, corners the camera does not turn, districts forever unknown to the ardent gaze – 'the random windows conjuring a street' as the poet has it. But which poet? You cannot remember. O grey world, you think, let me enter.

You go out halfway through the film, taking the back way past the lavatories, into a dim stinking passage that opens in a square beside a huge church in the familiar bourbon-biscuit coloured stone. The bells are ringing. The square is empty, the rain steady. To be here is like belief, amid this routine imminence: not now... not now... not now but very soon a sign will be granted. It is not that things will be made clear but that they will express the weight of an authority which has until now been discreetly but entirely withheld.

The rain neither slackens nor intensifies: but still. The bells fall silent as you skirt the church and cross a further bridge over a further canal into a park which turns out to be a graveyard. It is in fact a German military graveyard, a *Soldatenfriedhof,* for the town saw brutal fighting in one of the earliest phases of the Great War. Several hundred flat rectangular slabs extend across the marshy, mist-leaking lawn, like stepping stones. Beneath each stone are as many as eight men, inseparable in a single interment. The slow noyade of waterlogged earth completes the transition from corpses to phantoms. The outcome is embodied in the group of eerily still (well, of course they are still!) stone infantrymen at the far gate. As you pass beneath the arch it would seem entirely reasonable to notice headless, limbless, lipless figures standing or seated in the middle air, gazing straight through you, transformed by a grace of suffering you are hardly fit to read about. The very mildness of these unofficial angels, some of whom still bear their rusted weapons, is a reproof that History in its entirety could not face down. Do you see them? Not yet?

In the small square opposite the graveyard stands a fenced-in bust of a national poet of a century ago. He looks like a sawn-off Garibaldi in black marble, his stone book open blank before him, but the nationalism whose song he sang had little of liberty about it. His monument is to be ignored, for even in this place of obsessive readership and late-opening libraries there are probably no more than half a dozen people who could quote a line of his work or tell you his dates offhand. Only the illiterate care now for what they dimly imagine he said – about the Church, the corporate state, the Jews, the soil. The dead Germans in the *Soldatenfriedhof* did not know or care about him either. It is easy, in the presence of this parochial futility, to feel a disabling sense of exhaustion and to be drawn helplessly to sit on one of the green wooden benches and catch your death of something in the time-honoured manner. But you sense you are not finished yet. Still a little way to go, down the shuttered lanes in the slow gloom, through the halos of the gas-lamps, peering up at the occasional lit window to wonder at the life it houses and conceals. By now the evening has almost slipped away. People are going to bed with a book or each other, leaving herbal infusions to cool on the night table, hating the sight of themselves in the foggy inherited mirrors and turning up the corner of a page with a private criminal grin. They may even make notes in the margins, but only in pencil.

The next bridge marks a border. Here, in some way, at the outer ring of the canal, you leave behind the city proper and its spell of bookish near-sleep. Once across the bridge you could be anywhere, irrevocably. Over there, beyond the broad canal, lies the Lost Quarter, the deniable district. No wonder you hesitate, pretending to study the dark, rain-pitted water and its dormant barges wrapped in canvas, huddling at their moorings. But there was never any choice in the matter – you see that now. You, the pronoun, you syllable of breath, you were predicated on this crossing. It is where you, the subject, agree with the verb that has impelled you all along. You are lived, you are being been. You are language, completing its sentence without parole.

You go over. The curve of grey, steep-roofed, three-storey merchants' houses on the far side is no different from the street you are leaving within the ring of the canal, but none the less this might be another world you are entering. So this is the Lost Quarter, its settled quiet, its audible rain and obscure distances. This is the domain of Afterwards, where meaning goes to spend its retirement in harmless contemplation of all that it has lost. This is where, secretly, you have always wished to be. So: here is another dim lane between high garden walls, to one side overhung by a vast mulberry tree whose fruit lies crushed on the flagstones. It is as though this place is one more thing to remember, one thing above all, a birthright, a home, a passage of air through which you travel on the way to the lane's end – too late to pause, too dark to make out what lies before you now, but it is there, surely, a point to which you seem to be ascending slightly through the dark rainy air, forgetting and perfected as you go. A lifetime of faces is gone beyond recall. You have not brought a thing to read.

Notes

A number of these stories take place in what some readers may recognise as the Newcastle Literary and Philosophical Society Library, 'The Lit and Phil'. The building has been much altered in the telling, and no reference is intended to any members of staff, living, dead or otherwise situated.

Several pieces received their first hearing at 'Phantoms at the Phil', a bi-annual reading held in the library and organised by Chaz Brenchley. Thanks are due to him, to the Librarian Kay Easson and her staff, and to Gail-Nina Anderson.

'I Cannot Cross Over' was suggested by Antonio Tabucchi's *Requiem: A Hallucination* (Harvill, 1994).

'Close to You' was suggested by a passage on 'Carmilla' in Robert Tracy's Introduction to *In a Glass Darkly* by Sheridan Le Fanu (Oxford, 1993). I have paraphrased some of Professor Tracy's comments.

About the Author

Sean O'Brien was born in London in 1952 and grew up in Hull. He has published seven collections of verse: *The Indoor Park* (1983), winner of a Somerset Maugham Award; *The Frighteners* (1987); *HMS Glasshouse* (1991); *Ghost Train* (1995); *Downriver* (2001); *Inferno* (2006), his verse version of Dante's Inferno; and *The Drowned Book* (2007). The latter won the 2007 T. S. Eliot Prize. *Ghost Train*, *Downriver* and *The Drowned Book* have all won the Forward Poetry Prize (Best Poetry Collection of the Year), making Sean O'Brien the only poet to have won this prize more than once. His essays have been collected in *The Deregulated Muse: Essays on Contemporary British and Irish Poetry* and he was editor of *The Firebox: Poetry in Britain and Ireland After 1945*. He has translated Aristophanes' *The Birds* for the National Theatre, and dramatised novels for broadcast as BBC Radio 4 Classic Serials, including Yevgeny Zamyatin's *We* (2004) and Graham Greene's *Ministry of Fear* (2006). He currently lives in Newcastle.